Mary Coo[...]
July 24, 1918

$3.50

W9-CTQ-666

Brian

Jim

Honey

Mart

Di

Trixie Belden

Your TRIXIE BELDEN Library

Trixie Belden and the
MYSTERY AT
BOB-WHITE CAVE

BY KATHRYN KENNY

Cover by Larry Frederick

® A WHITMAN BOOK
Western Publishing Company, Inc.
Racine, Wisconsin

All names, characters, and events in this
story are entirely fictitious.

CONTENTS

THE MYSTERY
AT BOB-WHITE CAVE

Discovery · 1

"I HATE RAIN! It's simply pouring down, and it's darker than night outside."

Trixie Belden's usually merry blue eyes were rebellious. She pressed her face against the big picture window in her Uncle Andrew's fishing lodge, deep in the Ozark Mountains. Outside, rivulets of water ran down the glass. Thunder rolled in the distance, and wind whipped the branches of the pines and oaks on the rocky ledge where the lodge perched.

"It's *never* going to stop raining! Why did we ever come here?"

Mart Belden, fifteen, just eleven months older than his sister, looked up from the reel he was fitting to a limber fishing rod. "What's the matter with you? On the way here yesterday, you were so excited about everything you couldn't even sit still in the wagon."

"Yesterday everything was different," Trixie answered. "I'd never even seen a mule before, and then to ride the last few miles of our journey in a mule wagon driven by a girl my own age! The sun was so bright, and the hills were so beautiful. Who'd ever have thought we'd be drowning today?"

"Well, settle down. It won't kill you to wait out the rain. Try to get into the dart game with Jim and Brian."

"I hate darts!"

"Well, help Honey hem the curtains for the windows here in the lodge. You chose the material and had it sent out from New York, so get busy and help make the curtains."

"I hate to sew!"

"Gosh, go ahead and grouch, then, only keep it to yourself. If you could only see your face. It's worse than the rain clouds. You look so furious that even your hair is almost bright red."

"I don't care!" Trixie stamped her foot impatiently, and her short sandy curls bounced as if they, too, were impatient. "I wish Uncle Andrew never had invited us to come here. If we'd stayed home, we'd have been earning some money now for the new Bob-White project. That's what Dan's doing. We'll feel plenty silly if we have nothing to contribute toward the station wagon to take crippled children to the Sleepyside School. I hate this whole place!"

Trixie's older brother Brian stopped tossing darts for a minute. "That doesn't sound like you, Trixie. You're usually the best sport in the world. What do you suppose Linnie'll think of you?"

Trixie clapped her hand over her mouth and turned to Linnie . . . Linnie Moore, the daughter of Uncle Andrew's housekeeper at his fishing lodge.

"Oh, Linnie, I *am* a goop. I didn't mean a word of it. It's just frustrating not to be able to get out and do something. I never could stand to be cooped up."

"No one likes to be shut in, Trixie." Linnie's voice was quiet. "The rain will like as not stop just as suddenly as it started. It mostly does. What did you mean, though, about a station wagon for crippled children, and what is a bobwhite? I know you can't be talking about a real bobwhite bird. What is it?"

Trixie laughed. She had liked Linnie from the moment she had met her. That had been when the Ozark Mountain girl had waited for the Bob-Whites at the railroad station in White Hole Springs, Missouri. She had waited with the mule team and wagon that would take the visitors the last few miles of their journey from Westchester County, New York, where they lived, to the lodge in the Ozarks. No car ever could have traveled over the winding, rocky road.

"The Bob-Whites are us," Trixie explained. "Bob-Whites of the Glen. It's our club. Back in Sleepyside-on-the-Hudson, we have a clubhouse. We always have a project we work on as a group—something we try to do to give help where it's needed."

"That sounds wonderful. No wonder you're fretting now, with nothing to do. Is it a big club?"

"There's Honey, for one." Trixie put her arm around brown-haired Honey Wheeler, who sewed away patiently on curtains for the lodge. "Our clubhouse is on the grounds of her beautiful home. Then there's Jim, Honey's adopted brother, and my older brothers, Mart and Brian. Mart's not even a year older, but Brian's almost seventeen. Di Lynch is a member of the club, too. She's fourteen, the same age as Honey and me."

"Me, too," Linnie said.

"Di is out in California right now with her parents and twin brothers and twin sisters. Di is simply beautiful. Oh, yes, there's Dan—Dan Mangan. He's at home in Sleepyside, working for Honey's father's gamekeeper. Last and least, there's me. I'm sorry I was such a grump. I'm not always like that."

"No, she's not, Linnie." Honey spoke up loyally. "She's just the most wonderful—"

"Take it easy," Mart drawled. "She's far from perfection's prototype right now." Mart loved to use big words.

"I don't know what you're talking about," Linnie said, "but I like Trixie. I like all of you. Not many people around my own age come here. Mostly it's older people who come to visit your Uncle Andrew. Then I have to help Mama. There's lots to do around here—not today, of course, when it's raining. Except, it *is* getting on toward lunchtime now, and I'd better go and see if Mama needs me."

"She's sweet, isn't she?" Trixie asked Honey as Linnie left the room. "She's so calm. I'd give anything if I could stop getting so excited about everything."

"So would I," Mart agreed.

"It's this great, overpowering hunk of nature all around her that makes Linnie so calm," Jim said, "though we do have a good supply of nature ourselves back home, right in the lap of the Catskills."

"And with that big game preserve on Honey's father's land," Brian added.

"But none of it is as wild as this land is." Trixie picked up a magazine, riffled through it, then settled down near a table. "It was fascinating country that we came through yesterday. The mules practically stood on their heads coming down that steep road. I can't wait to explore it."

"There you go again," Mart said, disgusted. "Settle down and give the rest of us a break. Keep your nose in a magazine for a while."

Mart unreeled his line, wound it again, and made a short cast into a corner by the huge fireplace. "What's got into you now, Trixie?"

Trixie, her eyes glued to the pages she was turning, mumbled incoherently, the words tumbling over one another. Then she jumped to her feet, flapping the pictured pages dramatically. "Look! Just listen to this! See the funny ghost-white fish in this picture? Listen!"

The pictured fish looked like almost any creek fish, except that it was snow-white. Also, where its eyes should have been, there were only little rises covered with flesh.

Mart reeled in his line.

Trixie's brother Brian and his partner, Jim, left their dart game.

Honey looked up quickly from her sewing.

They were used to Trixie's bursts of enthusiasm, and they always paid attention to her. Life with her might be exasperating at times, but it was never dull. She had led them into and out of some mighty thrilling episodes.

"Listen!" she repeated, then read from the magazine. "'Biologists and other men engaged in medical research are showing great interest in fish found in underground caves. These fish, trapped by shifting earth or cavern breakdown, couldn't escape to the outside.'"

"So what?" Mart asked. "Why all the agitation?"

"Be patient! I'm getting to it. 'Because they couldn't escape outside, and because it was pitch-dark inside, gradually, through thousands of years, as generation followed generation, their eyes became mere mounds of flesh, then disappeared altogether.'"

"That's interesting," Mart agreed. "It isn't earth-shaking, though. Evolution is going on all the time. That's how human beings lost their tails. There are times when I could use a prehensile tail, I can tell you —when I'm playing basketball, for instance."

"This article I am reading is *very* important, Mart. *Please* may I go on?"

"Shoot! But make it a fast draw."

"The magazine goes on to say, 'Scientists want to make an intensive study of these fish, to determine the effect of environment on blindness and to observe how nature works to help animals adjust to blindness.'

"Now I'm coming to the part that's important to us. This magazine," Trixie said impressively, "is prepared to pay a reward of five hundred dollars for live specimens of Ozark cave fish in three stages of evolution—with fully developed eyes, with partly developed eyes, and eyeless."

Brian, a biology major at high school and intending to be a doctor, was instantly intrigued. "That sounds neat, Trixie. May I look at the article?"

Trixie handed him the magazine and jumped excitedly from one foot to the other. "Just think! Here we are, right on the scene. Doesn't it say in the article, Brian, that the fish are most likely to be found in caves in the vicinity of Lake Wamatosa? Well, isn't that Lake Wamatosa right down there below us? And doesn't it say that a representative of the magazine will be in White Hole Springs within a week or so? What's to keep us from going after those fish and presenting him with the three specimens he wants, *and*—" Trixie paused for effect—"collecting the five hundred dollars for the station wagon fund? If it would *only* stop raining!"

"What do you mean, 'stop raining'?" Mart asked. "When you were pointing out that window to Lake Wamatosa, you didn't even see that the sun is shining."

"Then let's start hunting for those fish!"

Mrs. Moore had been working quietly in the dining end of the big lodge living room, putting lunch on the table. Linnie, who had been helping her, had just brought in a bowl of salad.

"I think you'd better wait," Mrs. Moore said.

"Why?" Trixie asked, surprised.

"Because your Uncle Andrew isn't here."

"Don't you think he'd want us to go and hunt for the fish, Mrs. Moore?"

"I don't know. Exploring caves can be dangerous. Linnie knows that, don't you, Linnie?"

"It is likely to be risky," Linnie admitted reluctantly, "if you don't know anything about exploring caves."

"We do, though," Trixie said. "There's a cave in Honey's father's woods."

Honey laughed. "That old thing! We know every inch of it. There's certainly no danger there."

Mrs. Moore seemed worried. "Caves round about here have sinkholes in them. They have dangerous ledges and falling rocks. You could run into a wild animal or a snake. You probably would be perfectly safe, but I'd much rather you'd talk it over with your Uncle Andrew first. He'll be home for dinner tonight."

"All right. We'll wait till morning," Brian said. Brian was the conservative, dependable Belden. "Another few hours won't make much difference. You act as though you could walk right into a cave, Trixie, take the fish out with a dip net, and pocket the money. It

20

couldn't be that simple, or they wouldn't be offering a five-hundred-dollar reward. We'll wait, won't we, gang?"

"I wish we didn't have to waste a whole day!" Trixie said.

"You *are* on a rebellious kick," Mart said. "Why don't we go fishing after lunch? I'm dying to try out this reel. You bet me a dollar you'd catch the first fish. Don't forget that, Trix. If you don't go along, it'll cost you a dollar, because I'm going to get a bass. See if I don't."

"Oh, all right," Trixie agreed reluctantly. Then a thought struck her. A mysterious smile crept round her lips. It could be that they just *might* find a cave, and if they did. . . .

Uncle Andrew's lodge was built of logs. It was located deep in the Missouri Ozarks, where life was still quite primitive, but he had managed to have some comforts brought to his mountain home.

A great rough stone fireplace dominated one end of the big living room. The comfortable chairs and divans were of peeled hickory and had been made by the mountain people. Woven rag rugs covered the floors. From high above the lodge, clear, cold spring-water flowed by force of gravity through pipes to the kitchen and shower room. Hanging oil lamps provided mellow light for reading.

Uncle Andrew's bedroom was on the first floor in back, and stairs led from the living room to two large dormitories, equipped with comfortable bunk beds, on the second floor.

Through the wide-paned windows, where Trixie had watched the rain so impatiently, a glorious vista opened. Limestone ledges made a serrated pattern down to Ghost River, which emptied into the huge basin of Lake Wamatosa. Pines, walnuts, hickories, butternuts, papaws, dogwoods, redbuds, and wild crab apple trees tangled, in dense clumps, with wild grapevines and spiraling woodbines.

In a cleared place just beyond the lodge, Mrs. Moore's cabin stood. She had known no other home. Her grandparents had built the two-room log house when they migrated from Kentucky years before. After Linnie was born, Mrs. Moore and her husband, Matthew, had added a third room. From year to year, they had managed to clear a little more ground for gardening.

Ten years before, when Linnie was only four years old, Matthew Moore had gone on a fishing and hunting expedition. He never came back.

The evening before, after the Bob-Whites had unpacked and had dinner and Mrs. Moore and Linnie had gone to their own cabin, Uncle Andrew told them all he knew of the tragic affair. "The mayor of Wagon Trail," he said, "a little town south of Springfield, sent Mrs. Moore her husband's knapsack. With it was a letter saying that her husband's body had been found at the foot of a cliff, where, quite evidently, he had fallen to his death."

"How sad!" Trixie said. "It must have been dreadful if they had to bring his body here in that mule wagon."

"They couldn't bring his body home to be buried," Uncle Andrew explained, "because they had great difficulty in contacting Mrs. Moore. They did the best they could; they buried Matthew near where he had fallen. When Mrs. Moore received the letter and the knapsack, her husband had been dead for more than a month."

"What *did* she do?" Trixie asked.

"Here in the Ozark hills, people have learned to accept death stoically; when it happens, the family just goes on living. Mrs. Moore had to support herself and her child somehow. She gathered ginseng and other herbs in the woods and sent them with a neighbor to White Hole Springs, to be sent to city drugstores. She wove baskets, made pottery, and made dewberry and blackberry preserves. She carried her products by muleback, then sat patiently all day long by the roadside, hoping to sell them to passing tourists.

"She gathered wood and split it to keep Linnie and herself warm in winter. She canned vegetables and wild fruits. She shot squirrels and rabbits and canned some of them for winter use. She even managed to buy Martha, the cow, and Shem and Japheth, the mules. Things are a little easier for her now, since I was fortunate enough to employ her as a housekeeper."

The Bob-Whites quickly consumed the sandwiches Mrs. Moore had made, plus a big bowl of garden lettuce mixed with wild poke greens. There were little onions and radishes from Mrs. Moore's kitchen garden.

"Moms has lettuce and radishes in her garden at home," Trixie told Mrs. Moore. "Brian and Mart planted it for her, and they help her hoe and water it."

Mrs. Moore seemed surprised. "Then you all have chores to do at home. Do you hear that, Linnie?"

"I'll say we do," Mart said. "Plenty of them, the year round. Trixie helps Moms in the house with our little brother, Bobby, and with dusting and dishwashing. Brian and I have the hard work to do, though, washing Moms's station wagon and keeping Dad's car clean, working in the garden, and carrying in wood. Jeepers, we get the tough end of it, huh, Brian?"

"We have all the time we want for Bob-White work and basketball and baseball practice and skating," Brian answered. "You know that, Mart."

"Sleepyside sounds like a wonderful place to live," Linnie said, "especially your place, Crabapple Farm, and the Manor House, where Honey lives. I looked on the map in my geography. You're hundreds of miles from here when you're home. I've never been farther away than White Hole Springs. I wish I could fly in an airplane someday. That would be something fine. Did your mother teach you to sew, Honey?"

They all laughed at this question. Mr. Wheeler was a millionaire, and Mrs. Wheeler had servants to do everything for her. She enjoyed a busy social life far more than doing any work around her home.

"I learned to sew at boarding school," Honey explained. "I love it. I made these jackets we wear."

"They're beautiful, with your club name embroidered on the back and all. I can sew, too. From pictures I've seen in magazines Mr. Belden's friends have brought, and from the curtains you've made for the lodge, I know our cabin could be a lot prettier than it is. I wish I knew how to fix it up so it wouldn't look like all the rest of the cabins around here."

"It's clean and comfortable," Mrs. Moore said quickly. "What money it would take to change it we've had to save for your education."

Trixie's generous heart was touched by the longing in Linnie's eyes. "If you want us to," she said, "we can show you how to make things for your house, and they'll cost hardly a thing. The boys'll help, too. They're handy at fixing houses. You should see what they did to our clubhouse back home. The next time it rains, that's exactly what we'll do."

Linnie's face shone. "I may not have to wait very long. I don't think the rain's over yet."

"Gosh, then let's get going," Mart said. "I've *got* to give this reel a workout. Thanks for such a good lunch, Mrs. Moore. Come on, everybody. Linnie?"

"I have to help Mama this afternoon. Have a good time, but watch out for a storm. If one comes up, take shelter under a cliff. The rain crows are still crying rain. Hear them?"

"Right now there's not a cloud in the sky," Trixie said. "How could it be mean enough to rain more?"

"Do you have an insect spray?" Mrs. Moore asked.

"The mosquitoes and ticks are bad. And do you have heavy boots?"

"Yes, to the first question, and look at these boots!" Trixie held up her foot. "They're snake-proof. Anyway, even if we saw a copperhead or rattlesnake, Jim's Deadeye Dick with his gun."

"Don't step over your fishing line," Linnie called after them. "It's a bad sign. You'll never catch a fish if you do. Watch out for sinkholes. Watch out for caves. You wouldn't want to stumble into one!"

"Wouldn't I?" Trixie said under her breath to Honey. "Just give me a chance!"

Wildcat Comes to Call · 2

Jim whistled for Jacob, Linnie's black-and-tan coonhound. Then he and Brian went ahead down the precipitous rocky path to the lake. Mart followed close behind them. Trixie, impatient, was at his heels, pushing back the dripping, low-hanging branches of oak and hickory.

"Isn't this great?" she called back to Honey.

Honey's unenthusiastic answer was drowned in the hoarse cawing of crows, who protested human invasion into their world.

"Watch out for your old bamboo rod!" Mart called out. "Carry the big end and trail it after you. You'll put my eyes out."

"Oh, all right," Trixie said and reversed her hold

on her fishing pole. "One of these days I'll have a collapsible rod, too."

"Yeah, if you ever learn to cast. Where are you heading, Jim?"

"No place, yet," Jim called back. "Not till we get closer to the lake. Jeepers, this view is something, isn't it?"

Down below, a flock of white herons waded in the shining shallows, lifting their feet high. As the Bob-Whites neared, they rose up and lighted on tree branches that hung low over the water's edge. Soon, curious, they were back, spreading their wide wings and treading water. A big turtle scrambled awkwardly from a log and disappeared into the water.

To the right, lazy Ghost River, scarcely a dozen feet across, had carved a crooked channel through the hills to empty its water into the crystal lake.

"Just anyplace you look," Brian called excitedly, "you can see a place to fish. It's a bass fisherman's paradise."

"Let's wait and see. Linnie said fish never bite in a rainstorm," Mart answered.

Jim skillfully cast out his line and brought it back. Then he said, "Linnie is full of superstitions. For instance, Mart, she said never to step over your fish-line; it's bad luck. You just did it!"

"That's all gobbledygook," Mart said and stumbled across his glass rod, nearly knocking it into the water. The girls laughed at the consternation in his face.

"Not all Ozark superstitions are foolish, it seems,"

Jim said. "The people around here know a lot more than we do about snakes and wild animals—caves, too." He looked directly at Trixie. She just tossed her curls and pulled in her bobbing line. A ten-inch sunfish dangled at the end of it. The first catch!

"It's a beauty!" Mart called. "There goes the dollar I bet you. Me for a bass! See that log over there in the shadow? Everybody keep away from it. I saw it first." Mart, his rod and line working perfectly, made a brilliant cast. The froglike lure at the end of his line dropped down, hit the stump, then plopped into the water where it lay motionless. Slowly he twitched the imitation frog toward him. Suddenly the water exploded around the stump, and a bass rose from the foam, splashing with all its might. Skillfully Mart let out his line, drew it in, let it out, and drew it in, till the tired fish gave up. Mart pulled him from the water —a fourteen-inch largemouth bass!

The Bob-Whites gathered around to admire it. Then Brian, too, brought in a bass, and shortly Jim pulled one in.

"We haven't been here an hour, and look at the catch!" Mart cried exultantly. "Enough for two meals! Who said fish didn't bite after a rain?"

"What Linnie really said was that fish wouldn't bite *during* a rainstorm," Honey said. "She also said she didn't think the rainstorm was over. None of you have noticed the way the black clouds are piling up in the west. Don't you hear thunder? We'd better go."

Brian, the serious member of the Bob-Whites and

their acknowledged leader, took one look at the sky and issued an order to head for home immediately.

The sun had disappeared behind a bank of angry clouds. A wind came up through the silence—a silence more ominous than the rolling thunder which accented it. The sky in the west was a sullen green along the horizon. Tree branches, caught in the wind, swept low. Turtledoves stopped their cooing. Katydids and crickets no longer chirped, but the crows kept up their ratchety cawing. A frightened rabbit looked out from behind a bush. Jacob paid no attention to it but stood beside Jim, head down and tail between his legs, while the wind whipped his short hair.

The Bob-Whites scurried up the path. The wind increased its fury, and the rain came down in sheets. Lightning cut crooked paths across the sky. Trixie stayed close to Jim. Honey, her face white with fright, cringed under the sheltering arm Brian put around her. Mart, forging ahead up the steep path, came to a sudden halt.

"The wind has been here ahead of us. We can't ever get over this big fallen tree!" he cried. "What'll we do? The lightning is bad—real bad!"

"Around to the left! Deploy! Hurry!" Brian ordered. "And, Mart, no more alarms, please. There's no real danger."

"We'll find shelter as soon as we can," Jim called. He had hidden for days in the big Catskill woods back home, trying to keep out of his cruel stepfather's sight, before Honey and Trixie found him and Honey's parents adopted him. Skilled as a woodsman, he firmly took over from Brian.

"Straight ahead!" he called. "Keep going the way Brian started us, toward the cliffs overhanging the river! There may be shelter there. Hurry!"

They were all soaked to the skin, for the rain came down in buckets, undeterred by the heavy foliage above them.

Suddenly a haven opened up where the sandstone ledge on which they were walking curved past a cavernous opening.

"Get in there quickly!" Jim called. As he pulled Trixie to shelter and hurried the Bob-Whites inside, a big tree crashed near the entrance.

The inside of the cave was pitch-black. They couldn't see one another—couldn't see a thing except a faint blur of light through the cave opening.

Safe from the storm's fury, they shook themselves free of water.

Habitually, they never went anyplace without their flashlights, a lesson they had learned from experience in the Catskill woods. Now they shone their lights in circles to explore their surroundings. A room perhaps fifty feet long and fifty feet wide spread about them. The ceiling, high enough that they could easily stand upright, sloped toward the back till it reached the ground.

"It's just a big hole in a cliff," Jim said, "and a pretty lucky one for all of us, I'd say."

Trixie moved her light quickly over the damp clay

ground, along the side walls, here and there over the ceiling, then back again to the ground. Finally she held the beam on a corner in which a pile of bones stood out in the light.

Jim went closer to investigate. "I don't like the looks of this. They're bones of little animals—squirrels, raccoons. . . ."

"Probably trapped in here and died," Mart said. "Don't you think so, Brian?"

Brian moved closer. "No, I don't. I don't think Jim thinks so, either. We're in some animal's den."

"A catamount!" Honey cried. "Remember that one that scared us so in the woods at home? Let's get out of here. It'll be here soon, and we'll all be killed! Won't we, Trixie?"

"What did you say?" Trixie asked. Her mind wasn't on the storm or on a catamount or on a pile of bare bones. She was looking for a sinkhole where a "ghost" fish might linger. With her flashlight, she had hunted out every inch of the big room. "There's not a sign of water in here. I'll never find the fish here!"

"You *do* have a single-track mind," Mart said. "Did you even notice the storm before we came in here?"

"Of course I did, silly. I have a lot on my mind, though. If you don't want that reward money, I do. I'm not overlooking anything."

"I think this cavern is neat," Brian said. "Look at the way my flashlight brings out the color of the rocks!"

"Yeah," Jim said. "Gosh, look at this one!"

"I don't want all of us to be eaten alive, even if we *never* find a ghost fish or any more rocks," Honey said, shaking with fright.

She had been right at Trixie's side during most of her dangerous adventures, and she had promised to be a partner in the Belden-Wheeler Detective Agency, but she wasn't as fearless as Trixie, and she didn't pretend to be. "You take too many chances. One of these days you'll go too far, Trixie Belden. Do you think the storm could possibly be over? All those bones scare me, and I'm afraid of the wind outside."

"Bones can't hurt you, Honey. Don't be afraid," Trixie said reassuringly. "I think the storm may be over. I'll slip outside and see."

A few feet from the cave, Trixie stood looking about her. At her side Jacob suddenly lifted his head and stiffened. Trixie followed his eyes to the undergrowth above the cave opening. There, among the leaves, was a terrifying feline face, with long, gleaming teeth bared, ready to slash. Jacob braced his thin body and snarled. The wildcat growled its answer, its ears laid back menacingly.

Paralyzed with fear, Trixie tried to call out, but no sound came from her throat. The animal slunk closer. Jacob, with every hair on end, barked fiercely. The wildcat poised to spring. A convulsive trembling shook Trixie's body as, unable to make a sound, she awaited the wildcat's attack.

The smoothly muscled body hurtled toward the helpless girl—and a rifle shot rang out! The wildcat dropped to the ground, shot through the head, the wound clean and deadly.

Trixie, immediately released from her spell, screamed. Jacob circled her, barking. The other Bob-Whites spilled from the cavern and were horrified at what they saw. Honey, tears streaming down her face, clung to Trixie. White-faced, appalled, and silent, the boys stood before the big cat's body.

"Who shot it?" Jim asked.

Trixie shook her head. She didn't know.

"Hello there!" Jim shouted. His echoing voice was the only answer.

Her brothers' concern took the form of anger. "I could beat my head against the rocks for not realizing what might happen!" Brian said.

"Yeah," Mart agreed, "me, too. Look at that dog!"

Jacob sniffed the air, wagged his tail, then made off across the woods.

Trixie, somewhat recovered from her fright, lifted her head. A whiff of tobacco smoke drifted through the rain-washed air. "The person who saved me must be someplace close," she said. "Did you smell that tobacco?"

"Nope," Brian said and jumped to the ground from the cliffside where he'd been hunting through the brush. "Not a sign of anyone, not even Jacob." He shook his head, perplexed. "Why would anyone save another person's life and then just disappear? It beats me!"

"Thank heaven for his rifle!" Jim said.

Mart looked thoughtfully at the wildcat's stiffening legs. "The mystery deepens. There must be a big bounty on one of these skins. That alone should make whoever shot it come forward and claim the hide. How does he know we won't drag it off to get the bounty?"

"I don't know the answer to any of your questions," Honey replied, her arm still around Trixie. "I know one thing, though: I want to get back to the lodge as soon as we possibly can. Trixie has had a frightful shock. We have, too. Our clothes are soaked, and that wind is like ice."

"You're right," Brian agreed. He whistled for Jacob, who came running, his tail erect and waving. "Home!" Brian commanded. Jacob set off through the woods, baying lustily. Far south, another coonhound answered mournfully. Then another took up the cry.

"We can't go through that underbrush where Jacob went," Brian said, "but my compass says we're at least headed in the right direction. Try and find a path."

"Isn't that the way we came down?" Trixie asked, pointing to a stony, overgrown trail a few feet above them.

"It is! Smart girl, Trixie!" Jim said. "Well, we'll have quite a tale to tell your Uncle Andrew when he comes home tonight. Gosh!"

"We won't be able to tell him we found the ghost fish that editor wants," Trixie said sadly. "We've just *got* to go after those fish first thing in the morning!"

35

Ghosts, Ghosts, Ghosts! · 3

Mrs. Moore was waiting at the lodge door when the Bob-Whites returned.

"My, but I'm glad to see you!" she said. "It was a bad storm. I worried, even though Linnie said I needn't. She was sure you'd find shelter. I know, though, how helpless some of the people have been who have visited Mr. Belden. Linnie's gone off to pick up your uncle. They should be back soon. Mercy, you're all soaked through. You'd better get dry clothes. What's the matter, Trixie? You look so white. A snake didn't bite you, did it?" she asked anxiously.

"A snake didn't," Honey said, trembling with cold and still frightened. "A wildcat almost did."

"A what?" Mrs. Moore screamed. She hurried to

take Trixie in her arms and make sure she was all right.

"A catamount . . . a bobcat . . . a wildcat . . . whatever you'd call it," Jim said. "It was a fierce-looking cat as big as Jacob."

"Oh, my blessed Lord!" Mrs. Moore said and hugged Trixie tight. "A wildcat! An angel must have saved you!"

"Yeah, a ghost angel," Mart said, "who shot him right in midair as he was going for Trixie."

"A ghost?" Mrs. Moore asked, her voice trembling.

"Whoever shot that wildcat disappeared into thin air," Mart went on. "Trixie said she didn't see a soul —just smelled tobacco smoke. That was all. The way we figured it, he must have been a strange guy not to show himself. Jacob acted funny, too. After the wildcat was killed Jacob didn't growl or bark. He wagged his tail and shot off into the woods."

"A ghost!" Mrs. Moore repeated. "Jacob came home quite a few minutes before you did. I was uneasy about that. Thank heaven, your uncle will soon be here, Trixie. You're still shivering. No wonder, poor child! Don't you want me to go upstairs with you and help you get into dry clothes?"

Honey assured Mrs. Moore they'd be all right, but she held on to Trixie's arm as they went up the stairs. Halfway up, Trixie shook off Honey's arm. "I'm not so scared now," she said. "It was a narrow escape, wasn't it? I was so sure it was Jim who shot that wildcat."

"It would have been Jim if you hadn't dashed out

of that cave by yourself. You shouldn't have done that. You should have known it was dangerous."

"I just wanted to see if the rain had stopped. I wasn't hurt, was I?"

"You were awfully close to being killed, and you know it, Trixie. I'm not too sure I want to be a detective—not the kind who has wildcats jumping after her, anyway. I'd rather be the kind who would sit in an office and try to figure out who the mysterious person was who shot the wildcat."

They went on upstairs.

Trixie dipped her face in the basin of water that stood on their dresser; she threw her head back and shook water from her short sandy curls. "Yes," she said, thoughtfully toweling, "that is a real mystery, isn't it? Almost like a ghost. There! That reminds me of the ghost fish. Linnie said there are lots of caves around here, but if they haven't any more water in them than the one we were in today, they won't do us much good. I want to find those fish."

"I do, too, but I wish sometime we could just have fun when we go places. Mart said he wishes the same thing."

"Doesn't either one of you care anything about getting that station wagon? About helping crippled children?"

"There you go again. You know we do; we want it just as much as you do. But we don't want to work every minute and always have awful things happening. We'd like to have a little fun."

"We had fun fishing today, didn't we? I like to have fun, too, but I want to keep the search for those fish uppermost in my mind. Don't you think exploring caves is going to be fun?"

"It wasn't any fun today. I don't want to find any more wildcats."

"I'm sure that doesn't happen very often. Uncle Andrew didn't even warn us about wildcats, and neither did Mrs. Moore or Linnie. Instead, Uncle Andrew said that wild animals have pretty well left the Ozark woods—that they've been hunted and killed. He said they hardly ever see even a deer anymore. We see lots of them in your woods back home. Mrs. Moore said that only a few years ago, deer used to come up in her yard and feed with the chickens."

"How wonderful!" Honey, dressed in dry jeans and shirt, pushed back the new curtains she had hemmed and hung at their bedroom window. "You can see for miles," she said. "I believe that's the mule wagon coming up from the hollow. Isn't that it, Trix?"

Trixie looked, then called to the boys in the next room, "Uncle Andrew will be here soon. Let's go downstairs and wait for him; we'll help him unload the supplies."

When Linnie drove the mules into the yard and turned them expertly, just at the lodge's back door, the boys and Trixie and Honey were there waiting and waving. Jacob wriggled his body ecstatically and jumped onto the seat with his mistress.

"I see you're safe after the storm," Uncle Andrew

said as he handed the supplies into waiting arms. "Linnie told me you were off in the woods or down at the lake fishing. Did you have any trouble?"

"We sure did—" Honey started to say.

Trixie put her hand firmly over her friend's mouth and hushed her. "We'll tell you all about it later, when you're eating the bass we caught. What on earth is in all those boxes?"

"Take them inside, and before Mrs. Moore stows them away, you can see what's in them. What trouble did you have, Trixie?"

But Trixie had gone through the lodge door.

The boys unharnessed the mules for Linnie and led them to the shed. Mart was rewarded with a swift kick from Shem, while the other mule, Japheth, looked at him with a wild eye.

"A person never could get much attached to a mule, that's for sure," Mart said, rubbing his hip where the blow had landed.

"They're one-man mules—or one-girl mules," Brian said. "They're crazy about Linnie. She never even ties them in the shed. They'd never wander off from where she is; they just follow her around the way Jacob does."

The minute Trixie's uncle walked into the kitchen, Mrs. Moore told him what had happened to his niece that afternoon. His face drained white. He paced up and down the room, clenching and unclenching his hands. "That's one I didn't count on," he kept repeating. "When I invited you here, I thought you'd

40

not be in any more danger than getting your feet wet. You haven't been here two full days, and already Trixie has been attacked by a wildcat. Oh, Trixie!"

"I'm all right. I wish everybody would stop worrying. I'm safe. I'm alive."

"You just don't know these woods," Mrs. Moore said.

"I really can take care of myself," Trixie said quickly. "Back home we get in lots of tight places, but we always get out of them. Moms and Dad think we all have to learn to look out for ourselves."

"If you don't mind, since I'm responsible for you, I'll call the turns while you're here, Trixie." Uncle Andrew's voice was kind but firm. "I have a few bad memories, you'll remember, of how you went after the sheep thieves on my farm in Iowa. This is terrible!"

"She's off on another hunt now," Mart said. "She's after some ghost fish."

Uncle Andrew raised his eyebrows. "Ghost fish?"

So they told him all about the story Trixie had found in the scientific magazine.

"A five-hundred-dollar reward!" Trixie said. She went to get the magazine from the table in front of the fireplace. "Did you ever see a fish like this?"

"I can't say I ever did. I've never gone cave crawling, though. I just like to go after bass. That's my sport."

Conversation continued as Mrs. Moore put a delicious dinner on the table, but no one seemed able to eat much.

41

"Bass are all right to eat, and it's fun catching them," Trixie said, "but I'm dying to start hunting those ghost fish. I want to get up at dawn tomorrow and start. Just think . . . five hundred dollars toward a station wagon for crippled children!"

"I *am* thinking about it," Uncle Andrew said, "but I'm thinking more about the danger you'd run into if you tried spelunking. I'm still shaking from your run-in with the wildcat."

"Spelunking?" Honey asked.

"Of course!" Mart said, tilting his nose knowingly. "Amateur cave exploring, that means. Professionals are called *speleologists*. The science is *speleology*. It comes from the Greek word *spelaion*, meaning 'cave.' All kinds of scientists are interested in caves. Some of them want to find the sources of underground water. Medical researchers look for molds that may lead to new antibiotics. That editor," Mart explained to his uncle, "is looking for ghost fish in three stages of evolution—sighted, half-blind, and eyeless—so doctors can learn more about the effects of environment on blindness. . . ." Mart was breathless.

"Well, la-de-da!" Trixie said. "Where did you learn so much about caves and spe—spe—"

"Spelunkers? By keeping my eyes open, Trixie, and by reading instead of sleuthing."

"Never mind, Mart," Uncle Andrew said. "I'll have a lot to say later about this idea of cave exploration—I assure you. Now that we've finished our dinner, let's go into the other room. Mrs. Moore, too. Leave the dishes where they are. The girls will help after a while."

Uncle Andrew sat in his armchair in front of the fireplace and motioned to Trixie to sit on the ottoman at his feet.

"This is one of the things that bothers me," he said. "Speaking of ghost fish . . . I'd like to know first what ghost fired the shot that killed that wildcat." Uncle Andrew brushed his hand lovingly over Trixie's curls.

"We looked everywhere we could, and there wasn't a sign of him," Brian said. "Whoever got that big cat was a dead shot; that much we know for sure!"

Mrs. Moore sat quietly in her chair, twisting her hands in her lap. No one spoke for a while. Then she asked timidly, "Mr. Belden, do you believe in haunts?"

"Ghosts, you mean?" Uncle Andrew asked. He took his pipe from his mouth and smiled. "No, Mrs. Moore, I don't. There isn't any such thing as a ghost—though it does look as if a ghost saved my Trixie's life today, doesn't it?"

"*I* think so. Don't say you don't believe in them, Mr. Belden. They don't like that." Mrs. Moore's voice was very serious.

"No, sir." Linnie spoke up. "There are plenty of ghosts in the Ozarks. We know, don't we, Mama?"

"Yes," Mrs. Moore answered, then was silent.

"Ghosts?" Trixie asked, all ears. "Tell us about some of them. Maybe that *was* a ghost today," she added, "my guardian ghost."

"I think it could have been," Mrs. Moore said.

"Ghosts don't like being denied. They really haunt our mountains. Anyone will tell you that. Right down the hollow from here Mrs. Massey lived. Jake Massey's second wife she was, and she was mean to his children. She beat them. She didn't feed them right. One day— she told this herself—she was alone in the cabin, and a hard blow knocked her flat on the ground. Then she heard a voice say, 'Be good to those children!' She showed the red mark the ghost's hand made on her face. It changed her into a better mother."

"Hmmm," Uncle Andrew said.

"Tell us more!" Honey urged.

"Go on, please!" Trixie begged.

"I know of so many ghosts around here I wouldn't know where to stop," Mrs. Moore said. "There's an old cabin not far from here on the trail to White Hole Springs. Linnie will point it out to you. The people who once lived there murdered a stranger who stopped for a night's lodging. They stole the few dollars he had and buried his body out in the cow lot. He came back every night to haunt them. His ghost drove them out of these parts. No one will go near that cabin. If they did, they'd still hear him moaning."

"Didn't anyone ever have nerve enough to stay there?" Mart asked. "I would. I'd like to see a ghost."

"No one I know of ever stayed in *that* cabin, and you'd not stay long, either, if you heard that man moaning, Mart. Another place, though, an old man was murdered for his money. His ghost came back there, too, and people were afraid to stay in the cabin. One night a man who didn't know about the ghost was traveling through, and he took shelter there overnight. Toward morning he woke up and saw the ghost sitting by his bed. 'Follow me,' the ghost said, 'and I'll show you where they buried my money.'

"They went outside, and the ghost pulled some boards away from the cellar wall. The money was there, wrapped in some old rags. 'Give it to the poor,' said the ghost. But the man was greedy. He wanted the money for himself and said so. He told the whole story to one of the Cardway boys who passed the cabin right afterward. Anyway, he was going to town to put it in the bank, when the mule he was riding stumbled as he was crossing Ghost River, and the man was drowned. That's where the river got its name. They never found his body or the money."

"Jeepers, Mrs. Moore, you really do know about ghosts, don't you?" Trixie said, shivering.

"I do. I know many a story, and they're all true. The thing that bothers me all my days is that I've never had a chance to talk to the spirit of my husband—to find out how he was killed. There! I'd better get the dishes done. Do you want to help me, Linnie? No, sit still, Trixie and Honey. Mr. Belden wants to talk to you about the dangers of caves. At least, I hope he does."

The Bob-Whites drew their chairs close around Uncle Andrew.

"It's this way," he said. "I've no objection at all to your exploring any of the caves around here, and

45

there are many of them—all fascinating, I imagine."

Trixie drew a breath of relief and winked happily at Honey.

"However—" Uncle Andrew paused and looked intently at Trixie—"I must make a definite rule that not one of you is to go into any cave at any time unless he's with someone who knows all about this area's caves."

Trixie's face fell. "That takes away half the fun. A guide would just take us into sissy caves, like the one we were in today."

"It wasn't so sissy," her uncle reminded her.

"*Inside* it was, Uncle Andrew. There wasn't a sign of a crawlway or sinkhole or hidden stream or anything that even looked like a place where that editor said a ghost fish might be found. I want to go into some caves that haven't been explored."

"I'll not even object to that if you have a good guide with you. I think I know just the person, too—Slim Sanderson. He was born and raised around here, I believe. He helped Bill Hawkins build this lodge. He's probably around eighteen—young enough to be as adventuresome as you'd like, Trixie, but he should know this whole country and know all the rules of safe cave exploring. As far as that goes, I have a book here somewhere that tells the rules set down by the National Speleological Society. It's a small book with a red binding. See if you can find it over on the shelves, please, Trixie."

Trixie found the book and handed it to her uncle.

"Listen, please," he said. "These are the rules:

" 'One: Never go into a cave alone. Go in threes. If one person is hurt, someone can then stay with that person while the other goes for help.

" 'Two: Always leave word where you are going and when you expect to return. Leave a note outside the cave, telling the time you entered and when you plan to come out. Inside, leave a trail on the floor or on the cave wall, showing which way you have gone.

" 'Three: Always carry three sources of light—a carbide lamp attached to your cap, a flashlight strapped to your belt, and matches and candle stubs wrapped in oilpaper.

" 'Four: Never take chances. Extensive cave exploring should be done by experts, not amateurs.' "

"It's all sane advice," Brian said. "Is there more?"

"No. It goes on to warn spelunkers to be sure and get permission from the owner of the land before they explore a cave on the premises. No need to worry about that, though, because most of the land you expect to explore belongs to me. Oh, yes, there's something about the kind of clothing to wear and the special gear you will need. I think you all have stout boots, blue jeans, and sweaters. You don't have carbide lamps, though, so we'll go to town tomorrow and buy them and see if we can find some helmets to protect your heads from rockfall. And you'll need strong nylon ropes, too. I think the store in White Hole Springs will have the stuff. I'll get word to Slim at the same time."

"Oh, dear, that'll waste a whole day!" Trixie said

47

sadly. "Can't we just hunt around here close to the lodge first?"

"I'm sorry. No cave hunting anywhere without Slim, please. Especially after what happened today. Will that be all right with you?"

"I guess so," Trixie said reluctantly. Mart kicked her foot. "I mean . . . yes, of course, Uncle Andrew. But I just hope someone else doesn't get in ahead of us and win the reward."

A Trip into Town · 4

IT'S JUST LIKE the roller coaster in the amusement park at White Plains!" Trixie shouted as the Bob-Whites whooped and bounced while Shem and Japheth pulled them up the rocky incline. They were on their way to White Hole Springs to buy the equipment they would need to search for the ghost fish. Sometimes the road was little more than a path, and the wagon tilted precariously over limestone ledges that led to brush-covered hollows, how deep, no one knew.

A summer haze filled the air. The warmth of the morning sun scarcely penetrated the trees and close underbrush. A screech owl's mournful cry, loud and persistent, caught Trixie's attention, and she stopped bouncing and playing to listen. "There's the loudest stillness in these woods. No wonder you think there are ghosts around. It even smells like ghosts, Linnie."

"And what kind of a smell, pray, does a ghost give off?" Mart asked.

"Chilly and damp, like an old cellar—like that old house in the woods, where Jim's uncle lived. Don't you notice it, Uncle Andrew?"

"Are you sure it isn't my tobacco?" Uncle Andrew asked. He pointed with his pipe stem across the creek they were approaching. "It wouldn't be too hard to imagine ghosts around that old cabin, would it?"

Honey shivered and pushed closer to Trixie, who had stood up in the wagon to see better. "Gosh, what is it?" she asked. Around the dilapidated old log cabin a white mist swirled in spirals to form slowly moving draped figures. The mist then vanished into the clearer sky above the trees.

Linnie stopped the mules. "It's the cabin where the stranger's body is buried out in the cow lot. Mama said I'd point it out to you. Remember? That wasn't any screech owl you heard a while ago, either. It was the murdered man, still groaning as he did when they were killing him."

"Was he the one who went up into thin air just now?" Jim asked, teasing.

"Don't make fun of haunts," Linnie said solemnly.

"You don't honestly think there's such a thing as a ghost, do you?" Mart asked.

"Yes, sir, I do!" Linnie clucked, and the mules, who had been standing patiently, heads down and ears back, started up again. "And you will, too, Mart Belden, before you leave these parts. That cabin's haunted. Hold tight; we're going through the creek again!"

Jim and Brian, fascinated by the rock formations on either side, hadn't paid much attention to the talk about ghosts. Trixie had. So had Mart. Honey heaved a deep sigh of relief when they found the level road again and started uphill.

"I'd give a lot to see more of that ghost," Mart whispered to Trixie. "Shucks, it's nothing but old mist coming up off the swampy ground. Back home we see it a lot of times, don't we?"

"We call it will-o'-the-wisp," Trixie agreed, keeping her voice low. She didn't want to offend Linnie.

"Even the name always makes me feel creepy," Honey said. "If you and Mart plan to visit that cabin, just count me out."

The mule wagon rattled on. From time to time, small trails led off into the woods where ground had been cleared for family homes. Blue smoke rose lazily from rough stone chimneys. Hens cackled, announcing their morning offering of eggs. A cowbell clanked tonelessly now and then as a bony animal reached for tasty grasses.

"That's Bill Hawkins's place," Uncle Andrew said. "We'll stop there a minute, please, Linnie."

A neat cabin faced the road. Back of it, several acres of cleared ground spread, green with corn and other vegetables.

51

Linnie called, "Whoa!" and a group of laughing children ran out, seven of them, all ages.

"Hello, Linnie!" they chorused. Linnie answered, calling them each by name. Bill Hawkins hurried from the nearby field, and his wife came out of the house, smoothing her apron.

"It's near time we were eating; won't you stop and join us?" she asked hospitably.

"Pa killed some squirrels, and Ma made a potpie," the oldest boy said. "We'd like it if you'd stop." He shook hands with the strangers from New York. Then each of his brothers and sisters did the same, repeating their names as Linnie introduced them. "We haven't seen another girl since school was out," one of the gingham-clad little girls said. "Ma made dewberry shortcake, too," she coaxed.

"We're in a kind of hurry," Uncle Andrew explained. "These young people want to do some cave hunting, and we're on our way to town for some equipment. Another time, Minnie, we'll stop. Thank you for asking us. Mrs. Moore's the only one I know who can equal you for cooking. Come over soon, all of you, and sample some of it.

"Oh, by the way, Bill, I've sent for Slim Sanderson to come over to the lodge this afternoon to talk about acting as guide. I'll feel a lot better about the safety of these young people if someone who knows caves goes along. Don't you think that's a good idea?"

"Slim Sanderson?" Bill Hawkins's face sobered. He stroked his chin. "Maybe so. I guess so."

Regretfully the children climbed down from the wheel hubs, where they'd been standing, and Linnie started the mules.

"Give Slim a good talk about his responsibilities, Andy," Bill Hawkins called after them.

As the wagon neared town, the woods thinned out to scrub oak underbrush. The road widened, and the mules, sure of rest soon, showed greater evidence of life.

"We didn't see anything but the railroad station when we were here before," Trixie said, delighted. "The buildings are just like those on TV Westerns, aren't they?"

"I'll bet the place gets pretty wild on Saturday nights, doesn't it?" Mart asked Linnie.

"Linnie's probably never been in town on a Saturday night in her life," Uncle Andrew said, answering Mart's question. "I can tell you, though, that White Hole Springs is quieter by far than Sleepyside or any other small town in Westchester County."

"It's just like a stage setting," Trixie insisted. "There's the barbershop and the bank and—"

"This is the store," Linnie said. "I love to come to town." She stopped the mules, and the boys tied them to a hitching post, watered them, and put on their feed bags.

Inside the store, a tall man with stooped shoulders and a friendly smile greeted them. "He's Mr. Owens, the man who owns the store," Linnie explained.

Uncle Andrew shook hands and introduced the

Bob-Whites. "Sam's not only the proprietor of the store," he explained, "but he's also postmaster, sheriff, and part-time schoolteacher. He even does some doctoring."

"Jeepers!" Trixie said.

Mr. Owens ruffled her sandy curls. "It sounds like something, but it's a barrel of nothing," he said. "I've got a parcel of mail for you kids. Follow me."

He went behind a wicket labeled UNITED STATES POST OFFICE.

"It seems like your mom misses all of you," he said, examining each piece of mail before relinquishing it. "Your brother Bobby wants you to come back home."

Trixie's eyes widened.

"Oh, I always read the postcards. It's part of my compensation. There's someone else here from your state, stopping over at the motel on the edge of town."

"There is?" Trixie exclaimed. "Do you know his name? Is he a magazine editor?"

"Nosy as I am, I don't know the answer to that one. He wears glasses, if that helps."

"May we go right over and talk with him?" Trixie asked her uncle.

"And tell him what?" Brian asked matter-of-factly. "That you want dibs on coming up with the fish he wants?"

"We don't really have anything to say to him, do we?" Trixie said, deflated.

"We can do some scouting around and find out if he *is* from the magazine," Jim offered helpfully.

"I have to go to the lumberyard to order some lumber for that new room I'm going to build," Uncle Andrew said. "Then we'll go over to the motel for lunch. They have a restaurant there, and maybe the man who runs the motel will be able to tell us something."

"Like as not he won't," Mr. Owens said, his eyes twinkling. "He's the closemouthed kind. Me, I'm the bigmouthed one. What can I do for you?"

When they had bought nylon ropes, carbide lamps, short, thick candles, a box of kitchen matches, some small waterproof bags, first aid kits, and a sharp pickax, Uncle Andrew decided that the high leather boots they had brought from home would be adequate. "If a snake gets to you with those on," he said, "it'll have to hold the high jump record for snakes."

The store smelled of kerosine, licorice candy, gingersnaps in an open barrel, and new leather boots that dangled from a line above their heads. There were only a few other people in the store, and they stood politely watching the Bob-Whites. As the bundle of purchases grew, it was too much for one weather-beaten old woodsman. "What in thunder are they going to do with all that stuff?" he asked the storekeeper.

"They're going to do some cave exploring."

"There ain't a cave around here big enough to carry all that stuff into," the old man said. "And if there was, they might meet up with the devil himself. Better keep out of caves!" He waved a bony finger.

"Say, Pop, don't spoil my sales," Mr. Owens said. "Maybe that's what we've been needing around here —new blood that isn't frozen by all the scare stories about this country. Maybe we've got us a Mammoth Cave nearby, like the one they've got over in Kentucky, and these kids will find it. Good luck, young ones!"

"It's mostly Trixie's idea," Jim said. "She's pretty famous as a detective in Westchester County, New York."

The men burst out laughing and slapped their sides.

"You'll be laughing out of the other sides of your faces before Trixie and her partner, Honey Wheeler, ever leave this part of the country," Jim said solemnly and turned his head to wink at Uncle Andrew.

"He's right!" Uncle Andrew said vehemently and told the astonished men how Trixie and Honey, with the help of the other Bob-Whites, had uncovered the thieves who had been stealing his sheep back in Iowa.

"That's the best yarn I've heard in a long time!" one of the men said. "Have you got any more like it, Andy?"

Trixie just turned up her nose, took Honey's arm, and walked out the door. "We'll meet you at the motel," she called back to the others.

Jim, Brian, and Mart caught up with the girls a few minutes later. "Uncle Andrew was telling them about some of your other stunts," Brian said. "He won't leave till he has them believing you really are Sure-Shot Trix Belden, girl wonder of Westchester County."

"I just wish you and Jim and Mart and Uncle Andrew *would* let me have a gun and teach me how to shoot it," Trixie answered. "I'd show you!"

"Just let Moms hear you say that!" Mart said.

Trixie didn't answer him. "Do you suppose we can find out who that man at the motel is, Honey?"

"*You* can, if anyone can, and now's your chance to try. I don't believe there are many guests at the motel. There are only three cars parked here."

The office was vacant when they went in. After they had waited a short time, Jim whistled. No one answered. Trixie walked over to the desk, where a small bell stood. Before she tapped it, she noticed the open register. She squinted to read the signature scrawled across it in heavy black ink. Try as she would, reading upside down, she couldn't make out the name, but she did see, following the name, the printed words "Scientific Digest." She whistled triumphantly and motioned to the others to look.

Just as they were ready to leave, the motel manager came in and directed them to the small lunch counter down the hall.

"He's here!" Trixie said, elated. "The reward is really on the level. The magazine means business. Gosh, let's order our food in a hurry; order for Uncle Andrew, too. That guide, Slim, will probably be at the lodge by now. Let's get back as fast as Shem and Japheth will take us!"

"They're not astronauts," Mart drawled.

"Maybe they aren't, but they'll get us to the lodge,

and we can hike to the caves. I think there's almost as much to discover underground as there is in outer space. After all the money Uncle Andrew spent today on equipment for us, I'm going to try hard to show him it wasn't wasted. We're going to find those specimens. Right?"

"Right!" the other Bob-Whites chorused as the waitress came with the menu.

Getting Acquainted • 5

IN THE WAGON on the way back to the lodge, Honey gave Trixie a sharp nudge. "You haven't said a word for ten minutes. What are you thinking about?"

"I've been thinking," Trixie announced to all the Bob-Whites, "that we'd better keep the purpose of our exploration a secret. You can be pretty sure that everyone around here will be out after those specimens, once that editor at the motel starts talking."

"It sure won't be any secret then," Brian reminded her.

"No, but we'll have a head start of a few days."

"Slim will have to know what you're after if he's to be your guide," Uncle Andrew said.

"Will he really have to know?" Trixie's voice was

anxious. "He might possibly try to find the fish himself."

"If I know Slim, he'd rather go after a bass than after any cave fish. You wouldn't have to tell him there's a reward for the fish, would you?"

"No, I guess not. Do you know Slim real well?"

"I don't really know him at all, except seeing him around the lodge when he helped Bill Hawkins. He's some sort of relative of Mrs. Moore's, I believe. She said he's a regular woodsman; he's been running around wild since he could walk. If he's anything like Mrs. Moore, you can tell him anything and trust him completely."

"That's the best way," Honey said quickly. "I don't see any need to be so closemouthed."

"I don't, either," Mart echoed.

"Well, why don't we wait till we meet Slim?" Jim suggested.

"That's right," Brian agreed. "Trixie's intuition has worked more times than not. Let's see what she thinks of Slim."

Uncle Andrew, evidently impressed by the respect the Bob-Whites showed for one another, said, "It's up to you. Tell Slim or don't tell him. What I want him to do is to guide you and to point out any danger."

"Maybe we'll want to limit it to that," Trixie said, relieved.

Several times Brian and Jim asked Linnie to stop the mules while they looked at limestone and clay strata exposed on the jagged cliffs. They explained that each layer of different color represented an era in geological history, and they added that they wanted to do some exploring for minerals.

"You won't get a reward for that," Trixie said. "I'm in favor of devoting *all* our time to hunting the ghost fish."

"We can do both at the same time," Brian said quietly. "You forget sometimes, Trixie, about the rock collection Jim and I are trying to get together for the clubhouse."

"Some rock collections can be as valuable as fish specimens," Jim added.

"You're not serious, are you?" Trixie asked. "I never heard of anyone being offered five hundred dollars for a rock."

"It could mean more money than that," Jim answered, "if, for instance, we could find a deposit of celestite."

"What is celestite?" Trixie asked.

"A soluble mineral used in preparing strontium."

"All I know about strontium is that it has something to do with nuclear weapons."

"That's enough to know," Brian said. "We're not likely to find celestite, but it's only one of many minerals we *could* find when we gather rock specimens."

"Don't look so discouraged," Jim was quick to add. "We're really on the prowl for the ghost fish."

Trixie's face cleared.

"We're at the top of the hill that leads to the lodge," Linnie said, "but it's too late now to go cave hunting,

Trixie, even if Slim has shown up."

Slim *had* shown up.

When the Bob-Whites piled out of the wagon at the back door of the lodge, their future guide was half sprawling, half sitting on the porch step. He didn't change his position until Uncle Andrew invited him inside and introduced his guests from New York.

Even then, Slim stood looking down, one toe scraping the living room floor. He didn't offer to shake hands till the boys offered theirs. He didn't even look in the direction of the girls until Trixie stepped up to him and announced, "I'm Trixie, Brian and Mart's sister, and this is Honey Wheeler."

"Evenin', miss," Slim drawled.

He came to life, though, when the Bob-Whites spread their purchases around on the living room floor. The carbide lamps seemed to intrigue him. He picked one up, fooled with it a minute, then put it down. His eyes narrowed at the accumulation of candles, waterproof plastic cases, pickax, shining nylon ropes, and hard helmets.

"What do you aim to do with all this truck?" he asked.

"It's all gear that has been recommended by the National Speleological Society for cave explorers," Uncle Andrew explained.

Slim snorted, passed a worn, frayed rope between his hands, then picked up his lantern. "These are all anyone needs," he said. "See you in the mornin'. I'd figured to get goin' this afternoon, but it's too late now. Is eight o'clock too early for you dudes?"

Trixie bristled. "All of us *dudes* are strong enough and healthy enough to start out right now. We're ready if you are."

"See you at eight o'clock tomorrow mornin'," Slim repeated and ambled toward the back door. "An' go slow on packin' all that dude stuff along with you. I don't want to have to carry one of the womenfolk."

Trixie was speechless—that is, till she closed the door after Slim. Then she exploded.

"Do we *have* to go exploring with that—that—"

"Now, now, Trixie," Uncle Andrew said. "Slim's probably all right. He's just like any other young fellow around here would likely be—not afraid to grapple a wildcat with his bare hands and thinking all official equipment is sissy. Hold your ammunition for a while."

"I think first impressions are best," Trixie said confidentially to Honey when they went upstairs to get ready for dinner. "I've hardly ever been wrong on first impressions, and there's something sneaky and odd about that Slim."

"Oh, Trixie, I don't think so. If you think back, you'll remember several times when we both suspected people and were wrong about them."

"Name just one."

"Spider Webster's brother Tad. You thought the brother of our very favorite policeman in Sleepyside wasn't to be trusted."

"You thought so, too, at first."

"That's why we should both be more trusting."

"You don't catch criminals by being trusting." Trixie Belden of the Belden-Wheeler Detective Agency was talking. "All right, Honey, I'll give Slim the red-carpet treatment as long as he has it coming. Are you ready for dinner?"

At the table the talk reverted to Slim. All the Bob-Whites except Trixie had been amused at his attitude.

"Missouri is the 'Show Me' state, you know," Uncle Andrew said. "It'll be up to you Bob-Whites to show Slim you aren't dudes and can take the hardships of cave exploring as well as he can."

"Maybe we can't do it," Mart suggested. "The girls, anyway."

Both Trixie and Honey started to sputter, then realized that Mart was teasing them.

"I don't care!" Trixie said, her face red. "I just don't trust him completely."

Mrs. Moore passed a platter of crisp fried chicken to Uncle Andrew. "What's wrong with Slim?" she asked Trixie in a serious tone of voice.

"I don't think he likes us," Trixie answered.

"I doubt if he likes or dislikes. He doesn't know you. As far as trusting him is concerned, I've never heard of Slim having any brush with the law, unless it was for hunting out of season. Every man around here does that. They figure the woods belonged to them long before laws about hunting seasons were passed, and they have to hunt to eat."

"Do you think that your mistrust of Slim could arise from your insuperable aversion to any kind of supervised activity?" Mart inquired, lifting his mouth from an ear of buttered sweet corn.

"Maybe it could." Trixie surprised Mart so that he dropped the corn. "I guess I don't go for any kind of restraint. Uncle Andrew, I *am* anxious to find those specimens. I *am* eager for us to be the first ones who do find them, so we can get the reward and help the crippled children."

"I'm for you one hundred percent. Slim may eat his words, too, about the equipment. I wouldn't trust that frayed rope of his to hold up a two-week-old kitten, much less Slim. Well, let's forget him, and cave hunting, too, till morning. I'm going to go over some papers, and then maybe we can have some music in the living room. Linnie and her mother are quite a singing team."

Honey and Trixie carried the dishes from the table to Mrs. Moore in the kitchen. She separated the scraps that were to go to Jacob from those meant for the chickens and handed the pans to the boys. They carried them out, then fed and watered the mules. While the girls were helping Linnie and her mother wash the dishes, Mart and Brian took turns milking gentle Martha, who waited in the cow shed. Milking was one skill Jim knew nothing about. He played throw-and-fetch-stick with Jacob and then laughed amusedly as the coon dog caught a strange scent and went off into the woods, baying plaintively.

When the shadows fell and logs in the great fireplace crackled, Mrs. Moore drew down the hanging kerosine lamps and lighted them. Uncle Andrew settled into his easy chair with a sigh of contentment. "Is your guitar tuned up?" he asked Linnie.

"Yes, sir. I don't know what you want us to sing."

"One of your real mountain songs. That one about Peter Degraph. The song is called 'Come All Ye,'" Uncle Andrew explained to the Bob-Whites. "A man is about to be hanged for the murder of his sweetheart. He sings this song from the gallows as he protests his innocence. Sing it for us please, Linnie."

"If Mama will help me. I may need prompting on some of the words." She sang,

"Come all ye good people my story to hear,
What happened to me in the June of last year;
Of poor Ellen Smith, and how she was found
Shot through the heart, lyin' cold on the ground.

"It was my intention to make her my wife,
And I loved her too dearly to take her sweet life.
I never did think that we ever would part—
Now people all say that I killed my sweetheart.

"Yes, I choke back my tears, for you people all said
That I, Pete Degraph, shot Ellen Smith dead.
My love's in her grave, with her hand on her breast,
But the bloodhounds and sheriff won't let me have rest.

"My Ellen sleeps sound in the lonely churchyard,
And I stand on the gallows, heaven knows it is hard!
They're goin' to hang me. The law says they can,
But whoever hangs me hangs an innocent man.

"The man that is guilty had better beware,
 For my spirit will haunt him by land and by air.
 Some wild, scary night I'll come out of the gloom
 And send his mean soul bleeding off to its doom."

As Linnie twanged the last mournful notes on her guitar, something swished in the air outside and crashed, then rolled down the rough shingled roof. Terrified, Honey and Trixie jumped from their chairs. The boys turned and stood there motionless, listening intently.

"It was just a rock," Uncle Andrew said. "They break loose from the ledge up there and fall once in a while. It was timed just right, wasn't it? It really wasn't Peter Degraph's ghost, Trix!"

"Nobody knows it wasn't," Mrs. Moore said positively, a quiver in her voice.

Uncle Andrew chuckled. "You've never shown me a ghost yet."

"I hope I don't," Mrs. Moore answered. "Mostly they come to warn people of bad things that will soon happen."

Honey shivered. "Do you know any funny songs, Linnie?"

Linnie ran her fingers up and down the strings and began to sing in a lilting voice,

"Jaybird died with the whoopin' cough,
 Snowbird died with the colic.
 Met a froggie with a fiddle on his back
 A-goin' to the frolic.

> "He played fiddle dee dee.
> He played fiddle de fon.
> And the bees and the birds and
> The jolly little fleas
> Danced till the break of dawn."

Jim pulled his harmonica out of his pocket and caught the melody of Linnie's song, and they all clapped and stomped their feet in rhythm.

Suddenly the screen door snapped shut. The young people jumped to their feet. Trixie ran ahead and pulled back the curtain.

"I see someone—a dark shape out beyond the cow shed!"

In a moment Uncle Andrew was outside, rifle in hand—the Bob-Whites, Mrs. Moore, and Linnie close after him. They looked everywhere and saw nothing. Jacob came sniffing around Mrs. Moore's skirts, whining in the back of his throat.

"Jacob didn't bark!" Mrs. Moore said wonderingly.

"He wasn't here—just came in through the woods," Uncle Andrew said. "Are you *sure* you saw someone, Trixie?"

"She's always imagining she sees things," Mart said. "We were having so much fun. Let's go back in the house so Linnie can sing some more."

"Who slammed the screen door?" Mrs. Moore asked. "It didn't slam itself."

"It probably snapped shut with the wind," Uncle Andrew said.

Mrs. Moore looked skeptical. Trixie didn't believe

68

it at all. She was sure she really had seen someone outside. The mystery deepened when, as they finally went back into the house, Linnie found a little crippled bird on the back porch.

"Matthew always brought anything hurt home for me to look after," Mrs. Moore said. "It was his spirit was here. Oh, *why* couldn't I talk to him?"

"Nonsense, Mrs. Moore," Uncle Andrew said brusquely. "When the stone rolled off the roof, it hit the little bird, and it fell to the porch. It's simple. There just isn't any such thing as a ghost."

Mrs. Moore took Linnie by the hand and said soberly, "We'll bid you good night, Mr. Belden. Come, Linnie."

Upstairs, when they were getting ready for bed, Trixie cupped her hand over the chimney of the kerosine lamp, ready to blow it out. "Gosh," she said, "do you really think it could have been Linnie's father's ghost?"

"Who's the one with the imagination now?" Honey asked.

"Maybe it is imagination. I guess it is." Trixie climbed into her bunk. "But the queerest things keep happening here in these woods."

Swim to Safety · 6

I heard Slim ride up a while ago," Trixie said as she put on her blue jeans. "I suppose he's waiting for us downstairs. We'd better hurry. He doesn't think too much of *dudes*, anyway."

"It's only seven o'clock." Honey glanced at her wristwatch. "I thought we were going to forget about what Slim said."

"You're right. I'll forget it. The big thing is to get that reward. The last one down is a four-eyed catfish!"

Slim, at the breakfast table, answered the Bob-Whites' greetings with an unintelligible grunt. He'd just finished a plate of Mrs. Moore's cornmeal pancakes and wiped the syrup from his mouth with the back of his sleeve. "Ready?"

"When we finish *our* breakfast," Trixie answered, "and when we get our things collected."

"Where do you expect to head for first?" Mrs. Moore asked Slim.

"I been thinkin' Bascomb's Cave would be the likeliest place. Then maybe that old cave over near Turkey Knob."

"Are they caves that have already been explored?" Trixie asked.

"Sure they have. I've been through them dozens of times. Ain't nothin' there could hurt you."

"Are there underground streams in either one of them?"

"Never saw none."

"Then we won't go!" Trixie banged her fork down on her plate. It seemed to amuse Uncle Andrew. "Don't you know anyplace where we could find a cave that hasn't been explored?"

"Maybe about a couple dozen of 'em," Slim answered and took a deep swallow of coffee. "Trouble is, they might be too rough goin' for a tenderfoot. Wouldn't want to get too dirty. There's spider webs and bats and maybe a lot of slush and sharp stones in them."

"I guess we'd better have a little better understanding," Uncle Andrew said, aware of the Bob-Whites' growing impatience with Slim. "These young people may come from a different part of the country, but they can probably outswim you, outhike you, and, if you don't watch your way of talking, outfight you.

They can go anyplace you go and do anything you do. I just want you to guide them and obey rules that are just good common sense. I've already gone over them with you to refresh your mind. Do you think we understand one another now, Slim? I'm willing to pay you well to guide the Bob-Whites. They respect you and your skill as a woodsman. Give them the same respect for their talents. I think you may be in for a surprise."

Slim, who had reddened and bristled at the beginning of Uncle Andrew's conversation, changed his expression when reminded of good pay. He forced a grin. "All right. I'll call it quits if they will. I know my way around here, and I'm willin' to guide 'em. Never had no trouble before with guidin'."

"I think I know a good place for them to go," Linnie said timidly.

"Where?" Trixie asked eagerly.

"You'll have to take the boat. It's across the inlet after you pass the cove at the bottom of the path," she explained to Slim. "I was over there one day, and right under the cliffside, exactly kitty-corner from this lodge, there's the entrance to a real big cave. I don't think it's ever been explored. It's beautiful inside, just like a palace!" Linnie's eyes glowed. "I've only been just inside the entrance. There's a stream runs through it, too, Trixie. You might find a ghost fish there."

"What would you want with one of them skinny little things?" Slim asked.

72

"Then you've seen ghost fish in caves?" Trixie asked quickly.

"Once or twice," Slim said. "Gosh, what would you do with 'em? Now, if it's fish you're after, I know a place for bass."

"It isn't bass we're after," Trixie said, then added, "just now. I guess maybe Easterners are peculiar, don't you think, Honey?"

Honey nodded. She knew Trixie was trying to confuse Slim.

"Do you think we'll find any ghost fish in the cave across the inlet?" Trixie asked, trying to disguise the eagerness in her voice.

"As likely there as anyplace. But what in tarnation you want with 'em, I'll never know."

"That's as it should be," Trixie answered. "Let's go, Bob-Whites!"

She went into the living room, gathered up her bucket and dip net, put on her hard hat with the carbide lamp, and called a cheerful good-bye to Mrs. Moore, Uncle Andrew, and Linnie.

Then the Bob-Whites followed Slim single file down the winding path to the lake. He was as agile as an Ozark coonhound, but, slipping and sliding, they did manage to keep up. At the lake's edge, they threw their nylon ropes and other paraphernalia into the boat and climbed aboard. Slim and Jim took the oars. Mart pushed off from shore, then jumped into the aft seat.

"Here we go!" Trixie exclaimed.

Small waves rocked the boat, for a brisk breeze had come up. They sang as they went,

> "Row, row, row your boat
> Gently down the stream.
> Merrily, merrily, merrily. . . ."

"Heavens, what on earth is that? Someone's in trouble." Trixie pointed. "Look, Jim—Brian!"

Jim dropped his oar quickly and went over the side. Mart and Brian, then Trixie, followed. They knew they could never get their boat to the rescue in time.

A gray-haired man was struggling in the water beyond the cove, clearly losing strength. He had no chance of reaching his overturned boat. Jim swam like a water rat, while Trixie, with strong, even strokes, followed close behind him.

"Stay with the boat, Honey," Brian called back. "Pull it over here when we reach him!"

Jim, pushing himself at an amazing pace, reached the man first and tried to grasp the neck of his shirt to keep him afloat. Frenzied, the man put both arms around Jim's neck, pulling them both underwater.

Jim bobbed to the surface, gasped desperately for breath, and shook the drowning man like a terrier to try to loosen his spasmodic grip. Trixie, closing in, with the boys right behind her, grasped the man's fingers and twisted them to break his hold. He fought her with all his might, his face distorted in agony, but Trixie persisted, twisting vainly to free Jim's throat. Then, before Brian or Mart could help her, she drew back her doubled fist and brought it up sharply under the elderly man's chin. It struck with such force that at once the stunned man relaxed his hold.

It was a matter of seconds for Brian and Mart to take over. Mart freed Jim and began swimming back to the boat, pulling Jim's weakened body after him. Brian grasped the elderly man under his chin and swam with short, fast scissors kicks and a fast arm pull. After a few strokes, he slid his hand down across the chest of the inert man and towed him. Trixie then righted the man's boat, retrieved the floating oars, and pulled the boat through the water.

All of them converged on the lodge boat, which Slim, at Honey's urging, propelled toward them.

Trixie held the elderly man's boat still while Brian hoisted him in. He was already showing signs of returning strength when Brian took up the oars.

As the two of them headed toward shore, Trixie, her face reflecting the deep anxiety she felt for Jim, swam toward the lodge boat.

"What do you know, Trix?" Mart said as she climbed aboard. "Jim even swam part of the way here."

"It would take more than that to knock me out," Jim said huskily. "Don't think I don't know what you did, though, Trixie . . . all of you, for that matter. That man's arms are made of steel." He rubbed his throat.

"Back where you come from, does it always take three men and a girl to rescue a person?" Slim asked sarcastically.

"Back where we come from," Trixie answered coldly, "we don't draw straws when a man is drowning."

"If you mean why didn't I go for him, too, I'll tell you. With four of you in the water before I could say scat, I wasn't hankerin' for no swim. I figured, too, that a man with horse sense wouldn't go out in no boat lessen he could swim. I ain't no coward."

The Bob-Whites neither affirmed nor denied his statement. Paying no attention whatever to Slim, Trixie said, "We'll take the man to Mrs. Moore. She'll know what to do."

By the time they had beached the boat, the elderly man had regained some strength. "I think I can walk now," he told the Bob-Whites. "Sorry to be so much trouble to you all."

He couldn't really walk steadily, however, and the boys half carried him the rest of the way up the path to the lodge.

Mrs. Moore and Linnie ran out to meet them, and Mrs. Moore told them to take the man into the living room and bring pillows and blankets. For a while they were so busy getting hot coffee and hot-water bottles for the man that no one had a chance to explain what had happened.

When the revived man tried to talk, Mrs. Moore shushed him and directed the Bob-Whites to get into dry clothing immediately. Honey, who hadn't been in the water, could help her, and Linnie prepared some hot food while Uncle Andrew sat with the patient. "There's plenty of time to tell what happened," Mrs.

Moore said. "We don't want to add pneumonia to our troubles."

The Bob-Whites obediently started upstairs, talking and gesturing vigorously.

Slim had been leaning against the doorjamb. "I'll come back later if you 'uns want to try it again today," he said.

He was out and astride his mule before anyone could answer.

"I doubt very much that there will be another expedition today," Uncle Andrew said.

"Uncle Andrew, *please!*" Trixie begged from the stairs.

"We'll find out first what this is all about," her uncle said. "It looks as though a tragedy has been averted. That's no laughing matter."

"Everything's all right *now*," Trixie insisted. Then, when her uncle said no more, she followed her brothers and Jim upstairs.

The gray-haired man pulled himself up, threw off the blankets, and announced, "Everything is all right. How does a man even attempt to thank someone for saving his life?"

"What happened?" Uncle Andrew asked the man quietly.

"My name is Glendenning. I'm a visitor in this area. My home is in London. I have a variety of interests. I suppose you would call me an archaeologist or a geologist. Whatever the designation, there's one thing certain: I'll never be able to master a simple Ozark rowboat. It's as balky as the mules around here. I thought I was doing very well, when all at once I was catapulted into the water. I think one of my own oars saved me. I suppose, really, I'd be in Davy Jones's locker now if it hadn't been for the young people. It's always a question of whether a man's life is worth saving, but I've a wife and daughter back in England who may think I'm of some value. I say, how do I go about it now to row back to where I started?"

As the man and Uncle Andrew talked and Mrs. Moore, Linnie, and Honey bustled about preparing lunch, the Bob-Whites trooped down the stairs, no worse for their experience. Honey hurried to tell the others what Mr. Glendenning had told Uncle Andrew.

"It's wonderful to see you looking so well—" Trixie began but was stopped quickly by the man's rushing words of gratitude.

"You're no bigger than my daughter Gwen back in England," he said, then rubbed his chin, "but you pack a better punch! You're certainly a fine brave lass, and I thank you."

He took Trixie's hands in his and bowed. Then he shook hands with Honey, Jim, Brian, and Mart and warmly thanked them. "I owe you all a real debt. I hope I haven't spoiled your whole day."

The Bob-Whites, not at all at ease when they were being thanked for anything they did, quickly assured him that the best part of the day was still ahead of them.

This promised to be true, too, for Slim rode into

the yard just as they finished their lunch.

In spite of the Englishman's protest that he could find his way on foot to the cabin or row his own boat back, Mrs. Moore had persuaded him to let Linnie drive him. "I'm going up the road with her to take something to a neighbor who's ailing," she insisted. "It'll be easier for you to ride with us."

The Bob-Whites, sure that Mr. Glendenning was in good hands, again followed Slim down the path to the lakeshore.

Though their guide's code differed radically from theirs, and though they found it hard to understand his role in the morning's episode, by tacit agreement they accepted him for what he was—their guide but not necessarily their friend.

"Now, I wonder," Jim said as the boat was headed across the inlet, "just what that Englishman, clearly a cultured Englishman, is doing in this part of the world."

"You'll wonder no more," Trixie said sadly, "when I tell you something I saw. In the excitement of getting him to the lodge, I forgot to tell you. I saw it again just now. Do you know what Mr. Glendenning has lashed to the seat in that boat?"

"Out with it!" Mart said. "What did you see?"

"A dip net and a carbide lamp, that's what I saw," Trixie told him. "That Englishman is after exactly the same thing as we are."

Five-Hundred-Dollar Poison • 7

THE BOB-WHITES beached the boat at the foot of a limestone cliff that towered forty or fifty feet above, making a sharp, protruding ledge.

Impatiently, Trixie ran ahead up the shore. "Jeepers, did you feel that?" she shouted as a blast of cool air rushed out from under the center of the rock roof. "It's the entrance to the cave!" She pushed aside a curtain of vines and climbed over a pile of crushed stone that half filled the entrance.

"Just a minute, miss," Slim called. "Just a minute. There's things to be done. Jim, put that board up outside the cave and mark just what time we're goin' in and when we'll be out. It's downright foolish, but it's one of the things your uncle said to do."

Jim made a marker and set it up outside the cave. "It's about two o'clock now, and we'd better make it . . . well, say about four?"

"That's only *two* hours," Trixie protested. "What could we find in two hours?"

"All right," Jim said patiently, "let's make it five o'clock then."

"If you're goin' to spend three hours in every cave we go into . . ." Slim began, but he was talking to air, because Trixie was over the pile of rubble and inside the cave.

She couldn't see a thing ahead of her. There was only subdued light at the entrance, and beyond that, darkness. "Our carbide lamps! It'll take an hour to light the old things," she said. "Mart, please shine your big flashlight."

"We'll light our carbide lamps," Brian said authoritatively. "I'll show you how they work."

He took off his hat and lifted the lamp from the clamp. Then he unscrewed the two halves of the metal cylinder, poured water into the top half and carbide into the lower, and screwed the two halves back together. He set the valve in "on" position and waited till the water started dripping into the carbide. Acetylene gas, thus formed, escaped through the pin-sized hole in the concave metal reflector.

While Trixie fretted at the delay, she and the other Bob-Whites followed each step Brian made, then watched expectantly as he cupped his hand over the reflector to trap some of the gas and brushed his hand against the flint built into the inside of the reflector to ignite the flame.

Slim had lighted the stub of a miner's candle he had brought, but he couldn't keep back a shout of amazement when the lamps on the Bob-Whites' hats lighted the darkness.

The room where they stood was immense. All about them stalactites gleamed above stalagmites that rose from the floor beneath. On the walls, dozens of crystal formations came into view—draperies that flowed like velvet yet were stone, flowers that sent out delicate frondlike tentacles of limestone and sparkled in the reflected light like semiprecious jewels.

The ground under their feet was slippery with moisture, and the air about them was chilly. A stream trickled through the center of the big room, disappeared into a rocky crevice, and emerged farther on in a path it carved, only to disappear again under a cluster of limestone mounds.

"Haven't you ever been in here before?" Trixie asked Slim breathlessly. "Not even once?"

"Nope. There's nothin' in here you won't find in Bascomb's Cave I told you about or in the one at Turkey Knob. They're all alike, and I don't want none of 'em. If you've got any huntin' to do, let's start."

"Just a minute!" Trixie said. "I have an idea. This cave is on Uncle Andrew's property. It's a new cave. Does that make you think of anything?"

"Nothing but the fish we're after," Mart said. "What are you getting at?"

"Just this—a new cave should have a name." Trixie unscrewed the top of her canteen, poured water into it, held it up, and, as it dripped, said, "I christen thee—"

"Bob-White Cave!" they all chorused.

"Exactly! Isn't it wonderful?"

"Bob-Cat Cave'd be a better name," Slim said with contempt.

The Bob-Whites ignored him and searched the cavernous room with their flashlights. Time passed swiftly as they followed the stream, inch by inch, shining their lights on each ripple.

"Do you see anything?" Honey asked.

"Not yet, but I'm sure this would be the kind of place to watch. Was that a flash of white?"

The girls knelt on the rocky ground, the beams from their carbide lamps concentrating on the moving water. "Quick!" Trixie cried. "Right there under your nose. Jim! Brian! Mart! It's here!"

"It's not now," Honey said sadly. "I'm not even sure I saw it. Why didn't you dip it right out the instant you saw it?"

"It *was* there," Trixie insisted. "There it is again, right over there on the edge of the stream!" She reached frantically with her dip net, lowered it, and brought up a grayish, emaciated cricket from the water's edge. Its feelers were as long as its body, and the poor thing struggled weakly in the dip net.

"That's a fish?" Mart asked.

"You know it isn't," Trixie answered. "But where

83

there are ghost crickets, there are bound to be ghost fish."

"Let's get outa here!" Slim commanded.

Trixie looked at him, amazed.

"I don't hold with no kind of spirits—even fish spirits. The devil lives in caves. Anybody hereabouts will tell you that. Don't go beyond this here room, or you'll find that out. And them white things you see, in the water and out, they're evil. They're even poison!"

"Do you call five hundred dollars poison?" Mart demanded.

Slim's head went up. "Five hundred dollars?"

Mart, who'd been quickly shushed by four indignant Bob-Whites, just sputtered. "Forget it! Maybe they are poison, at that. We'd better leave 'em alone, huh, Trixie?" Mart walked over to the far wall and pretended deep interest in the formations.

"So that's it," Slim said half aloud. "Shucks, though, you was just talkin' big. Braggin'."

"When you know my brother better, Slim, you'll find out he spends a lot of his time doing just that— bragging." Trixie dipped her head to throw the light from her head lamp on the low edge along the stream. "Do you see those pinpoints of light?" she asked. "Is that some little animal, Slim? See it peeking around the edge of that shelf?"

"It's a pack rat," Slim said. "Like as not its nest is on that shelf."

"I don't like rats," Honey said, shivering. "Those big

old water rats near the Hudson at home are really dangerous!"

"Pack rats aren't the same thing at all," Brian explained. "They're as clean as squirrels and just as thrifty. They bring in their store of winter food and stow it away just inside the cave entrance. They're shy, afraid of humans. If you look down here on the floor, you'll see the tracks of their feet in wet clay. I read someplace that people trapped in caves have followed the tracks of pack rats to safety outside."

"Do you study things like that in biology?" Honey asked, always impressed by Brian's knowledge.

"Not exactly," Brian told her, "but I've been thinking that a person could do a lot of medical research in a place like this—molds, you know, and blind fish and crickets. It has lots of possibilities."

For the next two hours the Bob-Whites continued their search, hardly aware of the passing of time.

"How's about leavin' here?" Slim suddenly asked. "It must be gettin' toward five o'clock."

"It can't be!" Trixie said, aghast. "We haven't been here half an hour. I'm going on into one of those passages, the one where the stream leaves this room."

Mart held his wristwatch up to the light of his carbide lamp. "Not today you won't," he said. "It's not only five o'clock—it's already ten minutes past."

"Your watch is wrong!" Trixie said positively.

"It's right, Trixie," Honey said and held out her own wristwatch to show Trixie.

"Where *could* three hours have gone?" Trixie asked.

"This is the most fascinating place in the whole world. Can't we stay just another half hour?"

"Nope!" Slim answered.

"Jim? Brian?" Trixie pleaded.

"I said nope!" Slim snapped.

"Jim, is that Simon Legree our boss?" Trixie, incensed, inquired.

"When we're exploring caves, I guess he is," Jim said. "But take it a little easier, will you, fella?" he asked Slim. "I don't care for your tone of voice."

"Take it or leave it," Slim replied. "Everybody out, right now!"

Out of the cave Slim swaggered. He led the way down to the boat and, when they had all settled in, rowed briskly toward shore. Once there, he went first to Mr. Glendenning's boat, still beached on the shore, peered inside, and examined the bundle lashed to the seat; then he nimbly scrambled up the path, ahead of the Bob-Whites.

When they reached the lodge, Slim had already untied his mule and was riding off.

"Be here real early in the morning!" Trixie called after him. "We want to get back to the cave and have enough time to explore things. . . . Now, I don't know whether he heard me or not," she added impatiently.

"He'll show up," Mart said blithely. "It butters his bread. He sure had a peeve of some kind today, didn't he?"

"He has a perpetual peeve," Jim said. "If he keeps putting that chip on his shoulder all the time, one of us will have to knock it off."

"Not me," Mart said. "I wouldn't want to get in the way of one of his wallops."

"He's probably nine-tenths big talk," Jim said. "I believe he really thinks the devil lives in caves."

"I don't. I think he's cruel. I think he wanted to scare Honey and me. He seems to have a special hate for me."

"It's because you're a girl, Trixie, and you know a few things he doesn't. Who cares what he's like?" Mart held the lodge door open. "After all, he's just an indispensable adjunct to our ichthyological quest."

"Is that bad?" Uncle Andrew, chuckling, asked the Bob-Whites as they hurried through the open door and threw their gear in the corner.

"It's been a terrific day!" Trixie exclaimed as she dropped into the nearest chair. "Who ever even heard of such a day? We save a man from drowning, then find Aladdin's cave. It's the most marvelous cave in the universe, and we named it 'Bob-White Cave.' It would take all summer to explore that one cave."

"That would please me, all right," Uncle Andrew said. "I wish you *could* stay all summer. 'Bob-White Cave' it will be. I'll see that the name gets on the map in the engineer's office at the state capitol."

"Jeepers! Really?" Trixie asked.

"Really," Uncle Andrew promised. "So the afternoon of cave exploring was a success?"

"Only partly," Trixie said ruefully. "We didn't find the ghost fish. And, Mart, we never will get the reward if you keep sounding off about the five hundred dollars when Slim is listening."

Mart looked sheepish. "Don't worry about Slim. He didn't have any idea of what I was talking about."

"Don't be too sure of that. I wish I felt I could trust Slim one hundred percent."

"Was he a competent guide?" Uncle Andrew inquired quickly.

"Oh, he was that, all right," Jim said. "It's just his attitude—his arrogance."

"Maybe he feels you don't like him or trust him. If he's related to Mrs. Moore. . . ."

"He isn't, exactly." Mrs. Moore, setting the table, overheard the conversation. "He's related to my husband's cousin. Here in the mountains, it seems everyone is kinfolk to everyone else. I don't want you to think, though, that I've vouched for Slim in any way."

"Try to be a little more tolerant of him," Uncle Andrew urged. "Then if it doesn't work out, we can take it from there. Is that satisfactory?"

"Okay," Brian, the spokesman for the Bob-Whites, assured his uncle.

"Where is Linnie?" Trixie asked. "Oh, yes, she went with Mr. Glendenning. Did he feel all right when he left?"

"He seemed to have recovered completely. He didn't even want us to take him home in the wagon. He said it was only a 'bit of a way' to where he was staying. I thought, when he was trying to tell us where he lived, that he meant Dewey's cabin over near Turkey Knob.

It turned out it wasn't that at all. Here's Linnie. She'll tell you about it." Mrs. Moore's face was serious. "I just can't talk about it."

"Mr. Glendenning's living in that haunted cabin!" Linnie said in a low tone.

"By himself? He stayed there overnight?" Trixie asked. "Did he tell you he'd seen the ghost of the man who was murdered?"

"Oh, Trixie!" Uncle Andrew said, exasperated.

"Did he?" Trixie persisted. The other Bob-Whites looked expectantly at Linnie.

"No, he didn't. When he told me to let him out at the top of the knoll above the ghost cabin, I couldn't believe my ears. Mama and I told him to be careful when he passed there, and we asked him where he lived."

"What did he say then?" Trixie asked eagerly.

"He laughed and said, 'I live right there. The ghost takes good care of me. He'll give me a dose of herb tea tonight, and I'll be as good as new tomorrow.'"

"Then what did you say?" Honey whispered.

"I was so scared, I couldn't even say a word. Do you think Mr. Glendenning is a ghost himself? Mama does."

"Now, Linnie, don't go imagining things. The Englishman just liked to tease." Uncle Andrew seemed upset by more talk of ghosts.

"He wasn't teasing, was he, Mama? A person doesn't go right from saying their thank-yous to teasing you. I know he wasn't. And if you don't think he's a ghost or that he's in cahoots with ghosts, what do you think of this, Mr. Belden? When I was turning the mules around to come back home, I heard a dog bark. It was Jacob's bark. But Jacob wasn't anyplace around. I whistled for him. Still he didn't come. Then Mama and I saw the door of the ghost cabin open, and a man came out. . . ."

"Yes, Linnie, hurry up!" Trixie urged.

"He had a bag over his shoulder."

"What did he have in the bag?" Honey asked Linnie eagerly.

"He'd been poaching, probably, and bagged a rabbit," Jim said, remembering the game preserve around the Manor House at Sleepyside.

"He didn't . . . it may have been a—a—body!" Trixie said.

"Oh, Trixie!" Mart hooted. "What an imagination!"

"Are you laughing at me?" Linnie asked.

"Not a chance," Mart assured her. "Go ahead; tell us more about the ghost."

"Well, when the door opened, Jacob ran out, too. He ran like mad and jumped into the wagon."

"Gosh! Was the man you saw Mr. Glendenning?"

"No, it wasn't, Mart. The man I saw had a white cloud around his head. Mr. Glendenning seemed to fade out of sight."

"He'll be seen no more," Mrs. Moore said in a hollow voice.

"Oh, Mrs. Moore, I keep telling you—"

"I know, Mr. Belden—that there aren't any ghosts.

Wait till Linnie tells you the rest."

"Jeepers, is there still more?" Mart asked, finally impressed.

Trixie's eyes were as round as saucers and nearly as big. "Go on, Linnie, tell us!"

"As we turned the bend and looked back, we saw, flat against the wall of that cabin, the pelt of a wild-cat!"

When Linnie finished speaking, even Uncle Andrew had nothing to say. Mrs. Moore placed each knife and fork carefully on the table, all the while nodding her head knowingly. "Spirits," she said, half to herself. "Spirits at work."

Nothing but Trouble · 8

NEXT MORNING the clock in the lodge living room showed eight o'clock, eight thirty, then nine o'clock.

"What can be keeping Slim?" Trixie asked.

"Maybe he has chores to do," Uncle Andrew said. "There are many hours ahead of you."

"Where does he live?" Mart asked.

"I don't really know. Back in the woods someplace. Bill Hawkins knows."

"I wish he'd show up," Trixie said. "Other people may be ahead of us, hunting for those specimens. Mayn't we please go without Slim?"

"I'd feel much better if I thought he was with you. What do you boys think?"

"Slim's a pain in the neck," Mart said.

"But is he a competent guide? Do you think you'd be safe in that cave without him?" Uncle Andrew addressed his question to Brian.

"We know the cave pretty well," Brian answered. "At least, I think we do. I'd really like to try it with Slim another day, though. I just wish he weren't such an oddball."

"Do you trust him?"

"Yes, I guess so. Trixie doesn't, though, and she has a sort of sixth sense about people."

"Oh, why, why doesn't Slim show up, if he *has* to go with us?" Trixie asked impatiently. "Uncle Andrew, I *saw* those fish. I know I did. And the stream runs right through a great big room. Nothing could possibly harm us if we went by ourselves. Slim certainly wasn't any help to us in saving Mr. Glendenning. If we don't get to the cave soon, Mr. Glendenning will be there ahead of us. I'm sure he's after the blind fish, too. Don't you think we could go without Slim?"

"It won't be necessary to make that decision today. Slim just rode into the yard."

Down at the lake Trixie's sharp eyes noticed that the Englishman's boat had been picked up. "Now, who do you suppose took that boat?" she wondered aloud.

"Me," Slim said.

"When? Why? And why didn't we hear you going down to the lake?"

"I took it back last night, and I did it because the man asked me to. And you didn't hear me because I didn't think I had to stop and ask your leave to get the boat, Miss Nosy."

"That's enough of that!" Jim warned.

"Who says so? Want to make somethin' of it?"

Jim, who had seen the distressed look on Honey's face, didn't reply but shepherded the other Bob-Whites into the flat-bottomed boat and pushed off.

"It's pretty queer," Trixie thought. "Slim is afraid of ghosts, and yet he must have gone to the ghost cabin to see that Englishman. I suppose he offered to take the boat back if the man would pay him. There's something mysterious going on."

She forgot about Slim and his actions, however, as the boys beached the boat and they all went on to the cave. Inside, Bob-White Cave seemed even more wonderful than it had the day before.

Trixie and Honey swung their large flashlights to all four sides of the room. At the far end, the floor rose in a series of ledges, ending in a flat wall. The wall was an odd shade of brown. It looked as though it might be covered with moth-eaten bearskins.

"What is it, Brian?" Trixie asked.

"Bats. Thousands of them. They're asleep. Gosh!"

As Brian threw his light on the wall, it startled the bats, and, without warning, the bits of fur flew round and round. Then, like dive-bombers, they flew straight at the Bob-Whites.

Honey, terrified, beat them off. "Go away! They'll get in my hair, and I'll never get them out!"

"Don't be afraid!" Trixie said. "They won't hurt you.

That's a superstition—bats getting in people's hair."

"I don't care. I don't like them!" Honey wailed.

"They've settled down now, since you took your light off them," Jim said. "They're interesting. Bats fly by radar; did you know that?"

"At least they have their own warning signals," said Mart, who seemed to know something about almost everything. "They send out a high-pitched beep. Humans can't hear it."

"It must be something like the whistle we use to call Reddy back home," Trixie said.

"They seldom bump into anything," Brian explained further. "They send out those beeps, and the sound waves bounce back from any obstruction in their paths. When they fly, they screech at the rate of about thirty times a second. Aren't they something? I'd like to know a lot more about bats."

"Here's your chance," Slim said. "Wait'll you see what the buzzards and hawks do to 'em!" He picked up a handful of rocks and threw them against the far wall. The startled bats roared into flight, circling the cave clockwise and beating against the Bob-Whites, almost knocking them down. The girls waved their arms wildly and ran out of the cave. Slim, pushing the girls aside, ran ahead of them.

The whirring wings of the frenzied bats sounded like the roar of an express train as they found the exit. Outside, they flew in disorganized flight till hawks, flashing down from the sky, pounced on the helpless creatures.

The scene which followed was sickening. Trixie and Honey hid their faces as little brown balls of fur fell to the ground around them, dropped from deadly claws. The hawks were startled by the sudden appearance of the young people.

Gradually the bats escaped into the sky, and several ugly buzzards that had lurked on the outskirts of the fray, afraid to claim the little bodies on the ground, disappeared from sight.

"That was the cruelest thing anybody ever did!" Trixie said, her eyes flashing fire. "I hate you, Slim! Those poor little things!"

"Can we bury them?" Honey asked, trembling.

"We'll dig a trench with the pickax," Brian answered her.

When the grave was ready, the tiny victims were covered completely with sand, then mounded over with stones.

Slim watched the whole proceeding, evidently arrogantly unaware of the Bob-Whites' indignation. When the bats were buried, he spat contemptuously and announced to the sky, "Now I've seen everything."

"Not everything," Jim answered slowly, anger reddening his face. "You march down to the boat!" he commanded.

"Who says so?" Slim inquired belligerently.

"We do!" Brian said, backing up Jim. "We're through with you. March!"

Slim snarled viciously and came at Brian, head lowered. Suddenly he seemed to realize that he was outnumbered, so he stopped and swaggered down to the boat.

Jim and Brian, their faces stern, followed him. "You stay with the girls, Mart. Brian and I'll be back as soon as we deposit Slim's mean hide on the other shore."

"I *hope* that's the end of Slim," Honey said with a big sigh as the boat pushed off.

"It won't be," Mart said. "I think we'll have more trouble with him."

"He's mean, hateful, and cruel," Honey said and shuddered.

"You sure called the turn on him the first time you saw him, Trix," Mart said. "I guess Jim and Brian will go up to the lodge and tell Uncle Andrew about Slim and why we're through with him."

Mart, Trixie, and Honey extinguished their carbide lamps to save fuel and sat huddled on the beach, waiting for Jim and Brian to come back. Shading their eyes, they saw the boys put Slim ashore; they saw him turn on them and shake his fists, then go up the steep bank. They saw Jim and Brian go up the path to the lodge, then return, get into the boat, and shove off for the cave.

"Uncle Andrew said it's okay without Slim," Brian shouted from the boat. "Man, what a relief!"

"Hooray!" Trixie cried. "I feel as though Plymouth Rock has rolled off my chest."

Their carbide lamps again gleaming, the Bob-Whites reentered the cave. Brian threw a quick flash to the far wall, and they saw that some of the bats were still clinging there.

"They'll all be back tonight," he said. "They're just like homing pigeons. A guy at school told me that when the Pennsylvania turnpike was being built, a bat colony that had lived there for years just wouldn't leave. Workmen moved them to a nearby cave so smooth cement walls could be put in the old tunnel, but the bats kept flying back to roost in their old lodgings each night."

"I've had enough of bats for one day," Mart said. "Maybe you can continue your research some other time."

"Yes, please!" Honey begged.

Trixie had left the group and was crouched at the edge of the stream, her eyes searching the shallow water. "*Finally* we can hunt for the ghost fish," she said.

The other Bob-Whites walked carefully up and down the length of the stream that flowed through the big room. Once they saw another cricket on the rocks, and once Mart was sure he saw the flash of a white tail disappear under the rock where the stream left the room.

"We're just going to have to follow that stream," Trixie announced. "There must be some way we can do that. There's only a trickle of water here, and maybe in another part of the cave there's a real spring. I intend to find out."

"I saw a kind of funnel opening midway on this side

98

of the wall," Mart said. "Do you suppose. . . ."

Trixie was on her feet. Her light shining a short distance ahead of her, she followed the wall till she found a small opening.

"It's easy to crawl through here," she announced. "Here I go!"

Before anyone could speak, she lay flat on the ground and wriggled into the passage. Mart was close after her. "There's plenty of room," he called back.

"I can even see the opening ahead," Trixie's muffled voice announced. "Come on in, all of you!"

Brian had already entered the crawlway. Honey slid along after him, followed by Jim.

The passage, only about fifteen feet long, led to a room smaller than the one they had left. Here, however, they heard the rush of running water from a spring.

The ceiling was domed, exposing a dozen different strata—brown, orange, yellow, white, and a deep layer of black. The dome had the appearance of an upside-down pothole worn by some long-ago stream that had rushed with terrific force down through the cavern.

The floor was covered with fragments of limestone that had scaled from the dome and fallen to the cave floor. Iron, brought in by dripping water, had colored fantastic flowers and fernlike spirals that protruded from the wall and ceiling. Huge stalactites hung down, constantly dripping water that formed thick stalagmites or rimstones which cradled nests of calcite balls. It was a lovely fairyland, sparkling and scintillating under the searching lights of the Bob-Whites.

Trixie, usually sensitive to beauty, was so engrossed with her search for the fish that she didn't see the rock formations around her. Her hand clasping Honey's, she walked along the side of the stream.

Suddenly she let out a whoop, dropped to her knees, and brought up a ghost fish!

Mart came stumbling over the rough floor. Brian and Jim tore themselves from a study of the stratified dome to answer Trixie's cry.

"It's a fish! It's a fish! What shall I do with it? Where shall I put it? Oh, why didn't I bring the bait bucket?"

"Hold tight, Trixie, and I'll run for the bucket!" Jim said and vanished through the tunnel.

Trixie had the agonizing experience of watching a crayfish crawl by, followed by its ghostly brother, and still another before Jim returned.

Into the bait bucket went the fish. Then Trixie bent earnestly over the water. She snared a crayfish and added it to her catch. Concentrate as she would, though, not another ghost fish appeared.

The other Bob-Whites, eager to help, struggled over the wet clay, straining their eyes. Finally Brian announced, "It's almost five o'clock. We'd better go. Uncle Andrew'll be concerned if we don't show up soon."

"Oh, Jim, what shall I do with my ghost fish and my crayfish?" Trixie asked.

"I think it'll be better to leave the bucket right here, don't you, Brian?"

"Nobody asked me," Mart piped up. "Nobody thinks I know anything about cave fish. Any amateur spelunker would know that the specimens are more likely to survive captivity if they are kept in an environment to which they are inured."

"In other words, leave them here in the cave till tomorrow?" Trixie asked.

"Mart's right," Jim said. Brian agreed. So they inched their way back to the big room, Trixie pushing the bait bucket ahead of her.

"I don't know whether or not bats eat ghost fish," Trixie said.

Mart hooted. "They only eat insects."

"I'm not too sure you're right. To be sure, I'll buckle down the perforated top of the bucket, and my ghost fish and crayfish will be safe. And, jeepers, isn't the ghost fish a beauty?"

"It's the beginning of five hundred dollars' worth of beauty," Mart said. "It has those little knobs of flesh where its eyes used to be. We still have to find one with eyes and one without eyes or even knobs before we have a chance at winning all that prize money."

"I know that," Trixie said. "But this is a start. The other specimens are around here someplace, and we'll come back after them tomorrow."

Surprise Party • 9

THERE, THERE, NOW, what's all the excitement?" Andrew Belden asked as Honey and Trixie burst through the door, almost knocking him down.

"It's just that we found a ghost fish!" Honey called. "One of them. Trixie found it!"

"We *all* found it," Trixie announced breathlessly. "As soon as Slim was out of the way, everything clicked. I wish we could have found the other specimens, but ghost fish are rare. You don't just find them waiting for you around any old corner."

"Where is it? May I see it? Do you have it, Jim?"

Jim, Brian, and Mart had come in the back way and were talking to Mrs. Moore in the kitchen.

"We left it in the bait bucket in the cave," Trixie

explained. "We have a ghost crayfish, too. We thought the temperature in the cave would keep them much better."

"That was a wise thing to do," Uncle Andrew said. "Yes, what is it, Mrs. Moore?"

"See what I have. The boys found it at the back door—and not a sign of anyone around."

Mrs. Moore held a splint basket in her hand. She sat on a chair Linnie pushed forward for her and took off the cloth that had been laid over the contents of the basket.

"A dressed wild turkey," she exclaimed, "and two fat squirrels! Where on earth did they come from? It must be one of the neighbors who's coming here tonight—"

"Mama!"

"Oh, Linnie, what will you and Mr. Belden do to me? I didn't mean to let it out. It's a surprise party," she said to the Bob-Whites. "You might as well know it, anyway, because I never could keep it a secret from five pairs of bright eyes—two pairs of them belonging to famous detectives!"

"A surprise party! We just *love* surprises. Who's coming?" Trixie forgot her weariness from the cave explorations. Her eyes glowed with anticipation.

"We just let it be known around that we'd have a play-party tonight. The news goes from place to place, and we never really know who'll be here." Mrs. Moore got up to take the basket to the kitchen. "Now, wasn't it nice of someone to leave this offering? We'll have

103

our dinner right now, and you come and help me please, Linnie."

"Yes, Mama," Linnie answered, then added, "It's a good dinner!"

It was a good dinner. There were shelled garden peas cooked with scraped new potatoes. There were snap beans cooked with an end of salt pork. There was ham, just brought in from the smokehouse that afternoon, along with fried chicken and baked yams.

The Bob-Whites bowed their heads while Uncle Andrew asked the blessing, then ate as though they hadn't tasted food for days. "How could you possibly cook a dinner like this and plan a surprise party, too?" Honey asked.

"Linnie is a great help to me," Mrs. Moore said.

"Everybody's going to have to help now, though," Linnie said. "Trixie, if you and Honey will help Mama with the dishes, and if the boys will help me, we can be ready before the first person comes."

The girls hurried about, scraping dishes and dipping water for washing out of the big reservoir on the kitchen stove.

At Linnie's direction, the boys folded up the hooked rugs in the living room, pushed the furniture back, and brought in planks to put across chairs pushed against the wall.

"Will there be that many people? Will they have to sit on planks? Aren't there enough chairs?" Sitting on a plank wasn't Mart's idea of having a good time at a party.

"You'll see," Linnie answered. "The women Mama's age always sit along the wall and watch while we play games and dance. The men will play Pitch Up here in the corner. We'll put this table there for them. Jim, maybe you'd bring some of those camp chairs in from the porch."

Before long the whole character of the lodge living room had changed. It looked just like an old-time Western dance hall.

When the sun began to sink behind the pine-covered hills, the purple shadows lengthened, and Mrs. Moore pulled down the hanging kerosine lamps to light them. Then the first guests came. They were the Bill Hawkins family. The children, dressed to starched discomfort, got down from the wagon and waited, silently and timidly, till their father unhitched his mules, put feed in the wagon, and came up to the house. Then they passed single file through the doorway.

The Bob-Whites, glad to see the children, greeted the family warmly, and soon they seemed quite at home in the lodge.

One after another, other neighbors came, till soon the big room overflowed. Mothers lined up against one wall, as Linnie had predicted, babies in their laps, and chatted happily. In the corner, playing cards snapped as the men played their game. Young people the ages of the Bob-Whites clapped enthusiastically as the last wagon arrived and the musicians came up, one with a concertina, one with a guitar, and a third with a fiddle. The fiddler led a fourth man by the arm,

105

as he was blind, and half a dozen people ran forward to lead him to a seat. Blindness hadn't taken away his spirit, however, and he tapped his foot to the tempo as the musicians swung into a tune.

The man with the concertina jumped to the middle of the floor to summon young people for a dance. "First thing, we'll dance the hall!" he announced. Everyone began to stomp. The women cuddled their babies and stomped. The men at the card table stomped. The children playing around the room and in the kitchen stomped. Stomping to the tune, Jim led Trixie to the center of the circle which formed. Then, as Jim and Trixie danced, the circling couples clapped their hands and sang,

> "Lost my sweetheart, skip to my Lou,
> Lost my sweetheart, skip to my Lou,
> Lost my sweetheart, skip to my Lou,
> Skip to my Lou, my darling!

> "Skip to my Lou, skip to my Lou,
> Skip to my Lou, skip to my Lou,
> When you're through, remember my call,
> Change partners now and waltz the hall."

As the man with the concertina called the changes, Jim and Trixie retired to the outer circle and another couple took their place. This continued till all the pairs had "waltzed the hall."

In the kitchen, Mrs. Moore had pitchers of lemonade waiting, and Cokes were cooling in the spring. Linnie and Honey and Trixie carried trays of paper

cups to the older people in the big room, and the dance
started again.

> "Put your little foot,
> Put your little foot,
> Put your little foot
> Right there!

> "Take a step to the side,
> Take a step to the rear,
> Put your little foot right down,
> And forever stay near!"

For the laughing, shouting, dancing young people,
the musicians then bounced out "Black-Eyed Susie,"
"Sugar in My Coffee," and "Cotton-Eyed Joe."

"I wish the gang at Sleepyside High could hear
these boys," Mart whispered to Jim. "They really lay
it on the line, don't they?" And Mart, who had only
lately learned to dance, whirled out onto the floor with
Linnie as his partner.

Meantime, a big moon hovered outside the open
doors and windows, turning the outdoors to silver. In
the yard, Uncle Andrew busily swished about with a
spray gun, death to lurking mosquitoes and chiggers.
The boys started smudges going, then spread blankets
on the grass and took out several camp chairs for the
older people and one for the blind man.

When the guests swooped out of doors, the fun
went on. The dancing was over, but the blind man
borrowed the fiddler's fiddle, laid it across his knee,
and drew out sweet music to accompany his thin voice.

He sang ballads that found their way to the Ozark hills when English-born settlers came from the southern states; French songs that were inherited from *voyageurs* who explored the long rivers in far-off days and tarried to become the ancestors of the people who sat now in Andrew Belden's yard.

In the lodge clearing, tucked away in the friendly hills, a cool breeze came up from Lake Wamatosa while the people under the starlight sang and traded stories of witches and "haunts."

Mrs. Moore went into the house to make fresh lemonade and to bring out some cakes she had baked. Trixie followed to help. Everyone called to Linnie to sing, so, as her fingers swept minor chords from her guitar, she sang plaintively,

> "Oh, she was a lass of the low countree,
> And he was a lord of high degree,
> But she loved his lordship tenderlee.
> Sing sorrow . . . sweet sorrow.

"It's a song my father made up. Mother taught me to sing it," she said.

Somewhere, almost whispering, a man's low voice took up the refrain:

> "Sing sorrow . . . sweet sorrow."

He sang so low that Linnie did not hear him. No one in the listening crowd on the lawn seemed to notice. Trixie, in the kitchen, heard him and thought it was someone outside in the crowd. Jacob heard him and ran around in circles. Mrs. Moore heard the low refrain, paled, and gasped, "Speak to me, Matthew!" When no voice spoke in answer, she said sadly to Trixie, "It was Matthew's spirit. He brought that wild turkey and the squirrels. He's trying to take care of Linnie and me. He brought that little lame bird for me to tend, too."

"That isn't possible, Mrs. Moore," Trixie said. "Think back. It's only lately you've been thinking you saw your husband's spirit or heard it, isn't it? If he were going to take care of you, he'd have tried when Linnie was younger. I think you're so lonesome you just imagine things. One of the guests brought the gift as a surprise. That's the only possible explanation. I'll ask."

"You'll waste your time. No one in this world brought me the turkey and squirrels. It was Matthew's spirit. I know that for a fact."

Trixie shook her head. "But there *aren't* any ghosts, Mrs. Moore."

"You believe your way, and I'll believe mine. It comforts me, even if I can't speak to Matthew. Don't say you don't believe in spirits, either, Trixie. Honey told me about your Rip Van Winkle."

"But that's just a legend. No one really believes that it happened."

"More's the pity. Here in the Ozarks we *know* that restless spirits walk. I've seen things myself. I saw a white-covered corpse lying in the road. It was wrapped in a sheet. When I looked again, it wasn't there. It was just before they sent me Matthew's knapsack and told me he was dead.

"A woman I know rode over here one afternoon on her mule. As she rode, a baby floated in the air right alongside of her most of the way. She knew it for a sign and hurried to her mother's house, where her children were spending the day. Her baby had fallen off the bed and been killed. But there! I'll not spoil your party. Just don't ever tell me there aren't any spirits here in our mountains. Oh, I wish I could talk to Matthew!" Mrs. Moore dried her eyes on her apron. "Here's a pitcher of lemonade, Trixie. You take it out in the yard, please. I think everyone is ready for some more refreshments."

The children, stuffed to bursting and tired with playing, tumbled to sleep in the grass. Babies grew restless and cried. Men hustled to hitch up their mules. The women crowded around Mrs. Moore to thank her for the party and to invite her and her guests to "light and eat" whenever they were near their homes. Trixie and Honey picked up sleepy children in their arms and carried them to the wagons. The boys helped harness the mules. Then they all shook hands with the guests and stood laughing and waving as the crowd went off up the trail in back of the lodge, singing softly,

> "I have a Savior, gone to glory,
> I have a Savior, gone to glory,
> I have a Savior, gone to glory
>   On the other shore."

From the far top of the trail, where the lonesome road crawled crookedly through the trees, their voices came back:

> "Won't that be a happy meeting,
> Won't that be a happy meeting,
> Won't that be a happy meeting
> On that other shore?"

"That was a glorious party! I love every one of those people. I've never known anyone like them!" Trixie said enthusiastically.

Honey gave Mrs. Moore a hug and smiled lovingly at Uncle Andrew.

"You know how to give a real party, sir," Jim said.

"It was Mrs. Moore's idea—and Linnie's," Uncle Andrew said. "They did all the fixing for it."

The young people crowded around Mrs. Moore to thank her and pick up the last crumbs from the cake board. They watched her pack away the turkey and squirrels in the basket, to be taken to her cabin to cool in the cellar.

"Who brought them to you?" Mart asked.

Mrs. Moore didn't answer. A rooster crowed. "The wind's changed," she said. "Looks like we may have rain tomorrow. Linnie and I will bid you good night."

Upstairs, Mart called in to Trixie, "Who *did* leave the things for Mrs. Moore?"

"A ghost," answered Trixie.

"What did you say?"

"I said 'a ghost.'"

"Have you gone batty?"

"I'm not real sure. I heard the ghost with my own ears. Jacob saw him, or acted as though he did. Mrs. Moore is sure she heard her husband Matthew's spirit singing, 'Sorrow . . . sweet sorrow.' You heard all those ghost stories the people were telling tonight. They believe them. If I stay here long enough, I'll believe them, too. Right now all I can think of is that out there in that cave, we do have a ghost—a ghost that really isn't a ghost, yet it is. Oh, what am I saying, Mart? I'm so sleepy I can't think straight. We have to be up early in the morning to go back to that cave— Mart! What was that noise? Jim! Brian! Is that Linnie screaming? . . . It is! And Mrs. Moore's calling us. I smell smoke!"

Fire in the Night · 10

In the yard, pandemonium had replaced the peace of a short while before. The sharp, acrid smell of burning brush and wood filled the air. Smoke billowed from the level below, obscuring Mrs. Moore's cabin.

"My chickens!" she cried, wringing her hands. "They're shut up in the chicken house! The fire's making right for them. Jim! Brian! Trixie! Help save my chickens!"

The boys leaped over the ledge that separated the lodge grounds from the place where Mrs. Moore's collection of little buildings stood. They rushed to the chicken house and released the door catch, which had been firmly fixed against marauding skunks and foxes. Then, squawking and with feathers flying, the

113

chickens scurried out and disappeared in all directions.

Linnie hurried to the cow shed and led resisting, protesting brown Martha to higher ground at the lodge. The mules, never tied in their shed, were milling around the back lawn of the lodge, where Honey caught and tethered them.

Baleful little tongues of fire traced a definite path along the dividing line between lodge and cabin, eloquent evidence that the fire had been set—that it was meant to destroy the lodge. The wind that changed as the guests left sent the flames hungrily creeping in the opposite direction, to threaten, instead, Mrs. Moore's quarters.

Everyone rushed around frantically, beating out flames, carrying water, trying to save the cabin home. Trixie dragged the lawn hose through the kitchen to the hydrant where spring water came down from above.

"That's the girl!" Uncle Andrew called when she brought the gushing hose. "We *must* stop the fire before it reaches the underbrush on that slope. If it ever gets started up there, heaven help the whole pine woods and our neighbors' cabins."

The shouts and cries and the smell of smoke had brought the last of the departing guests hurrying back on the crooked trail to the lodge. Now these men and boys joined the fire fighters, while the girls, obeying Trixie's uncle, took the children inside the lodge.

"We'd better build a backfire over there forty or fifty feet this side of the underbrush," Bill Hawkins

114

cried. "That's our best chance. Bring some shovels, boys. Start here!"

Jim, Brian, and Mart, working with all the mountain men and boys, labored frantically, digging the backfire ditch and twisting sedge grass to kindle the opposing flames.

Frightened by the smoke and heat of the burning brush, little animals ran out across the level ground —small ground-nesting birds, chipmunks, skunks, a fat coon, and even a red fox. Jacob, who'd been racing about barking and getting in the way, took after the wild things and raced them up the hill toward the road.

Huge clouds scurried across the sky, and flashes of lightning crinkled around the horizon. The moon disappeared. The wind that had whipped up the flames subsided. But the rain did not come.

Mrs. Moore's chicken house burned like straw. The cow shed collapsed in a smoldering heap. But the fire fighters' quick, hard work saved the little home.

Now, if the backfire failed, the men well knew that most of their own homes would be lost in the flaming pines.

"Oh, *why* doesn't it rain?" Mrs. Moore moaned. The other women, trying to comfort her, watched the sky with anxious eyes. Thunder rumbled. Zigzag lightning illuminated the grim faces of the men who worked doggedly on. With tragic persistence, the fire, smothered in one place, flared up in another. Newly turned earth and backfire, which caught and was fanned to mounting flames, all seemed futile.

Now the underbrush beyond the backfire kindled and flared. Slowly the flames crept toward the ledge, where resinous pines rose against the sky. In the glow, a man's figure was silhouetted against the skyline. He appeared and reappeared, carrying buckets, pouring water. As the wave of flame advanced, the hose fell short by twenty feet, and the arc of water from it could not bridge the gap. With stolid tenacity, the men and boys worked on, relaying buckets of water, beating out the creeping fire, encouraging the growing fierceness of the backfire till they realized that it threatened finally to be as destructive as the danger it was supposed to avert.

Trixie, who had flattened her face against the living room windowpane, watching, could stand it no longer. In spite of her uncle's injunction to stay inside and mind the little ones, she turned them over to Honey and went outside to work side by side with Linnie and the men and boys.

It clearly was a losing battle. The scrub pines on the slope were almost a solid wall of fire. One by one, the fire fighters fell back—exhausted, defeated.

Then, as the first pine on the skyline flamed to a torch, the sky opened and the rain came. It came in sheets of water, quenching the holocaust as quickly and completely as snubbing a cigarette in an ashtray.

The men sprawled on the lodge lawn and let the rain drench them—too tired to move or talk.

Trixie, Mrs. Moore, Linnie, and the neighbor women

slowly walked to the house to prepare food and coffee. Honey had made pallets of quilts for the children, and they slept on the living room floor.

For a while the women and girls did not talk. Instead they cut bread, made sandwiches, opened cans of fruit, brought out cream and sugar, and heaped the kitchen table with food.

Slowly the men filed in, washed their sooty faces at the sink, then reached for sandwiches and cups of steaming coffee.

"That fire was set," one man said.

"For a purpose," another one added.

"I don't know who your enemy is, do you, Andy?" a third asked. "Do any of these young 'uns know?"

Trixie started to answer, but her Uncle Andrew gently stopped her. "If we do, we'll name no names until there is proof," he said. "When there is proof, there will be speedy punishment. Of that I'm sure."

"We ain't had a hangin' in this part of the mountains for many a day," one of the neighbors said, "but the devil that set that fire deserves to swing. When you decide to name names, Andy, there's those among us that knows how to take care of the scoundrel that threatened your home and ours. Now we'll get our kids and womenfolk together and get on."

"You won't go without my thanks," Mrs. Moore said warmly.

"And mine, too," Uncle Andrew said as he shook hands all around.

"We were fighting for the same thing, Andy," the

117

men assured him. "And we appreciate the play-party you all gave us tonight. If it hadn't been for that, we'd never been on hand."

"With no one here to help fight the fire, it would have been too late when the rain finally came," Mrs. Moore said, shuddering. "It seems now as though the Lord sent rain just for us, doesn't it? The sky's clear, and look at that moon! I hope the creek's not up so's you can't cross it."

"We'll manage," Bill Hawkins replied. "When you start rebuilding the sheds, let me know, Andy."

"That'll be tomorrow," Uncle Andrew replied.

"I'll be here, in the late morning."

It was nearly four o'clock in the morning when Mrs. Moore and the girls finished washing the dishes and setting things to rights. The smell of damp burned wood filled the air, reminding them constantly of the averted tragedy.

By common understanding, no one discussed the origin of the fire. "We'd better all get to bed now," Uncle Andrew said. "There'll be work to do tomorrow to clean things up, and there'll be things to talk over."

When the Bob-Whites went upstairs, Trixie couldn't settle down to sleep. She heard the boys tossing and turning in the next room. Honey, exhausted, slept restlessly, mumbling and moaning.

Trixie could hear her Uncle Andrew pacing back and forth, back and forth, downstairs. In Mrs. Moore's scorched cabin, a light burned.

Then Trixie slept.

Operation Fix-Up · 11

WHEN THE BOB-WHITES came down for a late break-fast, a sorry sight waited for them in the area around the lodge. The chicken house was completely de-stroyed, and the chickens were running wild. The ruins of the cow shed still smoldered. Nothing was left of the mule shed but a pile of charred boards.

Uncle Andrew's face was stern. "It's hard to believe that anyone would be so low as to deliberately set fire to someone's home. All the men seemed certain that the fire was set."

"It burned in such a straight line above Mrs. Moore's house," Jim said. "Fires don't burn that way unless they *are* set."

"We don't have to hunt far to know who did it.

Uncle Andrew, what are you going to do to Slim?"
Trixie asked.

"Nothing."

"Nothing?" Trixie cried. "After all the damage he
did to Mrs. Moore's home? You just have to take
one look at her yard. Her flowers are all burned, her
hollyhocks, daisies, four-o'clocks. They were so pretty.
Why, the fire even burned the vines on her porch."

"Thank heavens, it didn't get her home. I didn't
mean, Trixie, that whoever set that fire isn't to be
punished. I meant that I'm not the one to do it. Too
many Ozark men take the law into their own hands.
Here comes Mrs. Moore now. I hate to see this happen
to her. She hasn't had an easy life."

Mrs. Moore came in from the cold cellar, where
she'd gone for butter, cream, and milk for their breakfast. Her face was calm, but her eyes were red-rimmed
from weeping. "My chickens are scattered every which
way," she said. "I'll never get them together again.
And if I did, where would I put them? Oh, Mr. Belden,
your beautiful lawn! It's terrible."

"My lawn will be put in order in a short time. As for
the chickens, they'll sleep tonight in the new chicken
house the boys and I will build for you today. Right,
boys?"

"Right! We'll get started right after breakfast," Jim
answered. As soon as they had finished the hearty
meal, Jim got up from the table, and Mart and Brian
followed him.

"We'll use the lumber in the far end of the yard,"

Uncle Andrew said, "the lumber I ordered in town to build that new room off the kitchen. It isn't quite the right kind, but it'll do. We can put a stout door on the chicken house to keep out coons and skunks and foxes. There'll be enough material to build a shelter for Martha, too, Mrs. Moore. Don't fret. It'll all be done before you can say Kalamazoo."

Mrs. Moore put her apron to her eyes, then busied herself at the sink.

Trixie put her arm around Mrs. Moore's waist. "Honey and I are going out to your house now, to help Linnie clear up the damage there."

Mrs. Moore patted Trixie's hand gratefully and went on washing the dishes. "You girls and Linnie go ahead and fix the house up any way she wants."

Before the girls left, Bill Hawkins arrived to help Uncle Andrew and the boys. "Is someone living in that old ghost cabin, Andy?" he asked.

"I don't know, Bill. The boys and Trixie saved an Englishman from drowning out there in the lake. Linnie and Mrs. Moore took him home in the mule wagon. They sort of thought *he* was living there."

"Was he an old man with a billowy white beard?"

"No. Why?"

"I wonder. When we came over here to the play-party yesterday, we saw a man with the whitest hair I ever saw on a human. And he was creeping through the woods, going toward the ghost cabin. He had a pack on his back. My kids called him Santa Claus. He sure acted queer, as though he might be. . . ." Bill

121

Hawkins made a gesture toward his forehead to indicate that he thought the man might have been crazy. "Say, maybe—say, Andy, I told my wife a person would have to be crazy to set fire to this lodge."

Uncle Andrew looked at Trixie. "This whole thing will take a lot of investigation before the blame is laid on anyone. It's no use jumping to conclusions. Right now we have jobs to do. Trixie and Honey, you see what you can do to help Linnie. Bill and the boys and I will get busy with the sheds."

Mrs. Moore's three-room home was a sturdy log cabin. A porch covered the front of the house, and there was a hallway between the living room on one side and the bedroom on the other. Back of the living room, a kitchen had been added. Mrs. Moore's grandfather, who built the house, had taken pride in his work. He had built it of carefully selected logs, on a thick foundation of fitted rock.

Back of the kitchen, a cold cellar was built into the hillside. Inside were shelves of canned meat, fruits, vegetables, preserves, catsup, and pickles. There were jars of sweet butter and crocks of milk. Bins held diminished stores of apples, gourds, carrots, and beets from last summer's garden, still cool and quite fresh.

The fire had only singed the porch, but it had blackened the floor and cracked the windows. Later the boys and Uncle Andrew would paint the floor and repair the windows. "If Linnie wants us to," Trixie thought, "we can show her something we learned from those Four-H girls in Iowa—how to paint cans, fill them with flowers, and have hanging baskets all around this veranda."

In the living room the walls were pasted over with pictures from calendars. The fire had not reached the inside, but Linnie said, "I wish I could paint these walls. I'd love to have smooth walls like the ones in the lodge."

"That won't take long," Trixie said briskly. "That is, if you can find the right kind of paint. Let's go over to the lodge and see what's there. I know there's some of the soft pine-colored paint that Uncle Andrew used inside his place."

"I'd love that!" Linnie said.

They found far more paint than they would need and brought old newspapers with which to cover the floor while they painted. Soon all three were brushing busily at the walls.

"The paint has a latex base, and it'll be dry before your mother can even get over here to look at it," Trixie said.

"She's out telling your uncle and Mr. Hawkins and the boys what the chicken house has to have. She won't be in here for a long time. Isn't it the most beautiful thing you ever saw?" Linnie, brush in hand, stood off to look at a finished wall. "Even those old lace curtains'll look better when we put them back up."

"Would you like other curtains better, maybe some like those I made for Mr. Belden's living room?" Honey asked. "If you would, I think there's some material left. They'd be a little skimpy, but they'd look

123

better sill-length in here, anyway."

"That beautiful flowered material?" Linnie's eyes glowed. "Mama won't mind nearly so much having her flowers burned up, if she can have flowers inside the house. I can't wait to see what it'll look like."

"All right. If you and Trixie will paint the bedroom after you get through here, I'll get going on the curtains. It won't take long. They only have to be hemmed at the top and bottom. I'll measure the windows, then run over to the machine in our room at the lodge, and I'll have the curtains finished in a jiffy."

It was lunchtime before they knew it, and the girls followed Mr. Hawkins, Uncle Andrew, and the boys to the big kitchen table.

As Mrs. Moore went around the table pouring coffee, Bill Hawkins asked, "How's Slim turning out as a guide?"

Mart snorted, and, after a moment's hesitation, Uncle Andrew told Bill the whole story.

"That looks pretty bad," their neighbor said. "If you'll remember, I wasn't too sure about him. He's one of a big family, and his father and older brothers don't amount to a hill of beans. They're downright ornery. When they moved out of the mountains, Slim stayed behind. He always was a strange one, but I didn't think he was downright bad. Maybe he took to drinkin' moonshine or runnin' with some wild ones way back in the hills. If he set that fire, it won't take long for the men around here to take care of him."

"That's just why I don't want to mention his name.

I'd appreciate it if you didn't, either, Bill. I want Sam Owens to bring him in for a fair trial."

"You're a juster man than I am," Bill Hawkins said. "He didn't act fair settin' that fire."

"I'm not certain that he did it, especially after what you told me about the stranger over at the ghost cabin."

"But Slim might have been tryin' to get revenge on you for firin' him."

"It sounds logical," Uncle Andrew agreed, "but I intend to get the truth. There's been hanging done in these parts before when people weren't sure. I'm not going to be a party to such a thing now. Right at this minute, first things first. We'll get the work done here, and then I'll talk to the sheriff and see what he says."

"Have it your way. Feelin' flares up quick in the Ozark hills."

Uncle Andrew didn't say any more about Slim to Bill. "Your chicken house is up," he told Mrs. Moore. "All it needs now is a door to shut out animals that have a yen for chickens and eggs. Shall we get at Martha's shed now, boys?"

After they had gone, Mrs. Moore shooed the girls out of the kitchen. "I have to get things in order for dinner, and I'll do the dishes at the same time. Don't wear yourselves out over there at my cabin. I'm just so thankful it didn't burn that I'll not mind the cleaning up."

"Don't come over till we tell you, Mama!" Linnie warned. "We've got the most wonderful surprise!"

Linnie and Trixie finished painting the bedroom walls, then went back into the living room to hang some pictures. For her mother's Christmas present, Linnie had made a frame of hickory wood for her father's portrait. They hung it over the fireplace.

"I wish we had some of that pottery I saw at White Hole Springs," Trixie said, "the kind that's made here in the mountains."

"I have two vases in my hope chest in our bedroom," Linnie said. "I made them at school. I'll go and get them. Maybe you'd like to see my marriage quilts and other things Mama and I made," she added shyly.

"I'd love to. Heavens, you surely are getting ready for your wedding in plenty of time, aren't you?"

"It takes so long to make quilts. Don't you have a hope chest?"

Trixie shook her head. "I wouldn't have any idea about how to make a quilt. I guess Honey would, but I'm sure she hasn't started a hope chest, either."

"Every girl in the mountains has one," Linnie said proudly, and she threw back the top of the wooden box. "This is my Wedding Ring quilt. This is the Ozark Star. That's only *two* quilts, and I should have at least six. I have some hooked rugs, too. See, Trixie!"

"They're beautiful. Linnie, could we use the rugs in the living room right now? The dark green color of the floor would be a perfect background."

Linnie nodded, pleased.

"Then we'll put your darling terra-cotta vases on the mantel against the soft pine color we painted the

126

walls. Let's try it! I can't wait!"

"All right. First I want to show you my dream."

Linnie reached under some embroidered pillow-cases, brought out a school catalog, and opened it for Trixie to see.

"It's a catalog from the School of the Ozarks over at Point Lookout," she said. "Oh, Trixie, that's where I'm going to high school next year."

"And leave here?"

Linnie nodded. "Mama and I are going to Point Lookout soon to see the school and make arrangements. It's a far piece over there. It's the most beautiful school. See the picture of the dormitory where I'm going to live?" Linnie turned a page. "It doesn't cost some students one cent of money to go there."

"It doesn't cost anything?"

"Not if you have no money but a whole lot of ambition. Of course, now that Mama is earning money working for your uncle, she can pay some, but they'd have taken me, anyway. They said so. I just need my eighth grade diploma from Turkey Hollow School. My teacher told me about the School of the Ozarks. It's where she went to school, and she thinks it's really wonderful."

Linnie's words fell over one another. "Everyone who goes there works. The boys help maintain the buildings. They work with the cattle. They work in the dairy and make the ice cream they use in the dining room. They plow, cultivate the fields, and do everything else that the girls can't do."

127

"What do the girls do?"

"They wash clothes, make beds, help with the cooking, take care of sick people . . . everything . . . just about everything."

"How can they study and do all that work at the same time?"

"It's wonderfully planned. Everybody starts at seven o'clock in the morning, and they work and go to school till dinner time, six o'clock. You don't mind working when everyone else is working. My teacher said she just loved the school. Now they have a junior college, too. I want to be a teacher. Of course, I'll have to go to the University of Missouri before I can do that. But I may have a chance to get a scholarship."

"Where do they get the money to keep it up?"

"From people everywhere, people who give pennies and people who give thousands of dollars. I never dreamed I'd ever have a chance to go to high school, much less to college. I intend to work hard for that scholarship. It means everything in the world to me."

"I just know you'll win it!" Trixie said positively. "Won't your mother be proud of you! She'll—jeepers, Linnie, she'll be over here before we finish! Here's Honey with the curtains. Let's hurry."

The little room was transformed by the flowered draperies, hooked rugs, colorful bits of pottery, and newly painted walls.

"Those splint-bottomed chairs look so pretty in here," Trixie said as she stood off and looked at the room. "And the hickory tables, too. We'll help you

128

make some cushions later, so the chairs'll be more comfortable. You have such good taste, Linnie. It's a dear little house."

"You and Honey have made it that way."

"Oh, no, we didn't. All the ideas were yours. We just helped."

"I know Mama'll think it's just beautiful," Linnie said, gazing about the room dreamily.

She did. She thought it was so beautiful that she cried. Then they all laughed because each one of them had tears in her eyes.

"Rest now," Mrs. Moore said. "Bill Hawkins has gone home, and the boys and your uncle are stretched out on the lawn. You girls rest. There's time before dinner. The chicken house is rebuilt. So is Martha's shed. Shem and Japheth can wait for their shed."

"I wish we knew how that fire started," Trixie said as they went out the door. "Slim is mean enough and cruel enough to have done it. When the boys ran him out after he did that terrible thing to the bats in the cave, he looked so vicious—as though he'd like to murder all of us. He's the only person I can think of who'd be wicked enough to start the fire."

"Yes, but I keep thinking about that ghost cabin," Honey said.

"That is a mystery. If it hadn't been for Slim's meanness, we'd have all the specimens we need right now to get that reward. Specimens!" Trixie cried. "Gosh! I forgot all about them. Mrs. Moore, do you suppose we'd have time before dinner to row over to the cave and check on them? They might have suffocated or starved in that bucket."

They were walking across to the lodge as Trixie was talking. Jim overheard what she said about the fish and jumped to his feet. "It won't take more than a jiff to give them the once-over," he said. "Come on, gang."

The Bob-Whites hurried down to the boat.

Uncle Andrew had just settled down with his before-dinner pipe, when he heard Trixie shouting as she hurried up the hill from the lake.

"It's gone!" she said as she burst into the living room. "The fish is gone. The crayfish is gone. Even the bait bucket that held them is gone. That Slim has been there! He wasn't satisfied to burn down everything. He had to steal our fish, too."

Uncle Andrew laid his pipe on the table. "Did you *see* him take the fish?"

"No," Trixie answered, exasperated, "but, Uncle Andrew, we saw him going around the bend in a boat. That Englishman, Mr. Glendenning, was with him. If you look down there between the trees, you can still see their boat—see? It's pulling in at the foot of the ghost cabin. Now can we put Slim in jail? He's been trespassing in Bob-White Cave and stealing things that belong to us."

"I'll see about it tomorrow," Uncle Andrew said.

"Oh, my beautiful fish!" Trixie wailed. "I *hate* to wait till tomorrow to try to get it back!"

Search After Dark · 12

SOMETHING SCRATCHED against the window outside. Trixie, in her bunk next to Honey's, sat up straight, listened, and heard it again. "It's nothing but an old branch rubbing against the eaves," she said to herself, "but I *can't* go to sleep."

Then she heard a door close softly downstairs. She struggled from the covers, looked over at Honey, saw that she seemed fast asleep, then slipped into her shirt, jeans, and sneakers. Quietly, stealthily, she went down the stairs.

She flashed her light around the room. Linnie and Mart, huddled beside the fireplace, dropped to the floor, trying to conceal themselves. "Oh, it's you, Trixie," Linnie whispered. "I'm *so* glad you haven't gone. I knew at dinner time you'd try to go to that old cabin after the ghost fish tonight. I didn't want you to go alone."

"I had the same idea," Mart said. "I thought I heard someone downstairs, thought it was you, then found Linnie. When your light flashed, we were afraid we'd wakened Uncle Andrew."

"We'd better be real quiet, but I don't think he can hear way over in his room beyond the kitchen," Trixie said. "I'm glad you're going with me." *Isn't this neat?* she thought to herself. *I'd just about given up the idea of trying to find that cabin after dark.*

"What I really hoped was that I could talk you out of going," Linnie whispered. "It's dangerous in the woods at night."

"You told me it was dangerous in the woods in the daytime, too. I really intend to go, Linnie, so, please, don't try to stop me. You'd better get Jim's rifle, Mart."

"He won't need to; I have it myself," a low voice answered from the foot of the stairs. Jim came into the ring of Trixie's flashlight. Back of him came Brian and Honey.

"If you're going, so are we," Honey said. "I brought your boots, Trixie."

"Jeepers, thanks!" Trixie sat on the floor and laced up her high boots as quickly as possible.

They closed the living room door softly behind them. Outside, Jacob rose, stretched himself, and padded along after Linnie.

"For goodness' sake, don't let him bark!" Trixie

warned. "If he were to wake Uncle Andrew. . . ."

"He'll be as quiet as any of us if I tell him to be." Linnie stroked the big hound's ears.

She led the Bob-Whites along the corkscrew trail winding through the ravine that paralleled the river and skirted the lake. To follow the mule trail to the ghost cabin would be to run the risk of alerting every hound from the Stacy family's Old Blue to the Jenkinses' Jethro.

They kept their flashlights trained on the ground. Overhead, the sky was polka dotted with stars, and the moon sent little bypaths of silver through the tangled underbrush.

The frogs in the marsh by the river sang their *roua-roua-rou*, some tenor, some bass, and some that just snapped off in a hiccup. The katydids kept up a constant, high-pitched, blatant chorus. "I can't even hear myself think, they're so loud," Trixie complained. "Your mother said to tie a knot in my handkerchief and they'd stop. Wait a minute."

"Oh, that's to stop a whippoorwill," Linnie said. "You bang on a tree to quiet katydids. Try it, Jim."

Jim banged with the toe of his boot, and the clamor in the trees above stopped. It stopped in the next tree, too, and on and on, in a wave of silence that was more ominous than the racket of the insects.

"Someone has been along this trail recently," Trixie said. "See the broken branches? I smell tobacco smoke, too."

"Yeah?" Mart said. "Your imagination's working

133

again. Why would anybody—what's that?"

A branch snapped nearby, followed by a rustle in the leaves.

"It was an old coon—no, it couldn't have been, or Jacob would have been after it. What was it, Jacob?" Linnie asked. Jacob just wriggled his body and wagged his tail. "It must have been some animal—a red fox, maybe, on the way to Mama's chicken house. Thank goodness, the chickens are safe. I mean, thank you, Jim and Brian and Mart."

"Doesn't Jacob go after foxes?" Mart asked, curious.

"Not when I have hold of his collar," Linnie answered.

The trail turned sharply upward, and the Bob-Whites followed Linnie over rotted tree trunks and through knee-deep beds of dead leaves collected in gullies. On a level piece of ground near the top of the ridge, a stream swollen by the recent rain rushed toward the river and lake far below.

"There goes our visit to the ghost cabin!" Jim said. "We'll drown if we try to cross that. I'll bet it's full of sinkholes a mile deep. Remember those gullies we just crossed?"

Linnie stepped gingerly to the edge of the rushing water. "I think we can cross it," she said, "though I've never before been up here after a rain. Come, Jacob! Can we cross?"

Jacob plunged into the water and half paddled, half scrambled to the other side.

"There's our answer," Brian said. They crossed without any trouble. "Good dog, Jacob!" Brian rubbed the hound's back.

"The cabin shouldn't be far from here now," Linnie said. "Wait, Trixie!" Trixie, impatient, fell back to let Linnie lead through the tangled grass, ferns, and wet leaves.

In the clearing ahead of them squatted the old log house. Moonlight played across the sagging porch. The deeply set windows looked out like great staring eyes. Across the valley in back of the cabin, a star trailed across the sky, and a screech owl whimpered in a nearby tree.

Suddenly a rifle shot spat through the trees above the Bob-Whites, and they fell to the ground.

"Don't move!" Jim commanded.

"That shot came from the woods," Linnie said. "Oh, I wish we'd stayed at home. No good ever comes from spying on a ghost."

"Shhh!" Trixie cautioned. "Someone is coming over the rise toward the cabin!"

"It's nothing human!" Linnie said in a choked voice. "It's floating in a white cloud, just like we saw that other time, when we were on our way home from town. Oh, I *wish* I hadn't listened to you when you tried to tell me there aren't any ghosts."

"There aren't, Linnie!" Trixie said in a loud whisper. "Watch!"

"I can see a shape walking. It's all wrapped in white," Linnie said. "If it isn't a ghost. . . ."

"It's a man!" Jim said. "A man with a huge growth

135

of snow-white beard. And his hair looks like Einstein's
. . . or like Israel's former prime minister's. What's his
name?"

"Ben-Gurion," Mart answered. *"Non fatuus per-
secutis ignem."*

"We're half-murdered and you quote Latin," Honey
said. "Mart, don't you have any fear—"

"Of spirits?" Linnie finished the sentence.

"All I said was 'It is no will-o'-the-wisp I have followed here,' " Mart said, "and it isn't. That old guy is
real. He has a pack on his back, too, just like the man
Bill Hawkins said he saw. There's your thief, Trixie,
and the arsonist, too."

"All that is very interesting," Brian said, "but what
was his motive?"

"Who knows? Maybe it was some old feud. I think
Slim is mixed up in it with him. Where the heck did
he go?"

"Into thin air," Linnie whimpered, "just like any
ghost. It's the same ghost Mama and I saw when we
took the Englishman home when he nearly drowned."

"It *wasn't* a ghost," Jim said, "and I think he was
going someplace right now to hide the loot he had in
that bag."

"That loot is probably my ghost fish," Trixie said,
"in the bait bucket. But where did he go?"

"Into some cave, maybe," Mart said. "Let's keep
our eyes open for him."

"Let's keep our eyes wider open for the person who
shot that rifle," Trixie said.

Just then it cracked again.

"It's someone hunting squirrels," Linnie said.

"At night?"

"They do, sometimes."

Trixie was not convinced. "Then explain to me why a number-one coon dog like Jacob wouldn't flush a squirrel."

"Didn't you hear him panting to go after that noise? I still have him by the collar."

"Don't let him loose, then, or we're dead ducks," Mart said.

Just then Jacob pulled free and dashed off into the woods, wagging his tail expectantly.

"Come back here, Jacob!" Linnie called. "Oh, dear, maybe I'll never see him again. The ghost will get him!"

"The 'ghost' isn't home now, that's for sure," Mart said. "I feel like a cat at a mousehole. Say, Trixie, do you want to take a closer look now that the 'ghost' is away?"

"I want to find my fish, but I think the 'ghost' is hiding it."

"Let's take a look around, anyway," said Mart eagerly.

"Look out!" Linnie cried. "That big black dog—it's the ghost's dog. He's set it to watch for us. You never can kill him, Mart, or frighten him. Don't try. A person could throw an ax right through a ghost's black dog, and it wouldn't budge."

"That's a black dog?" Mart asked. He threw a rock.

It sailed through the air, hit the "black dog," and ricocheted into a clump of bushes.

"See? You couldn't kill it!" Linnie wailed. *"Please, let's go back home."*

"Stop teasing her!" Trixie commanded Mart. Then she put her arms around Linnie. "It's nothing but an old black stump. Turn your head around. You can see it plain as day in the moonlight. Here's Jacob, too. You didn't need to worry about him. That man has gone off into the woods; he doesn't know we're here. Let's just take a quick look into his house and see what he's up to, and then we'll take the mule trail home."

Linnie stepped forward bravely after Jim and Brian. "All right, if you say it's safe," she told Trixie.

Slowly, single file, the Bob-Whites stole up to the side of the house and stood in the shadow.

Trixie raised herself on tiptoe and peeked through the window, flashing her light. It traveled over the stone fireplace. Strings of pumpkin and wild onion hung from the mantel, drying. Fagots were piled on the hearth below. On the far side of the room a little cot stood, neatly made up, and beside it were an old kitchen chair and a rickety table with a kerosine lamp.

When Trixie started to draw her light away, she saw something that made her gasp. Just inside the door, off to one side, stood a bait bucket.

"It's mine!" she cried. "Just look at it! Someone who lives here stole my fish. Maybe Slim lives here. I

138

never heard anyone say where he *does* live. I *wish* I could go in there and get my fish!"

"That's one thing I won't help you to do, break into someone's house," Jim said positively, "and no other Bob-White will, either."

"I wasn't going to break in. I only said I wish I could get my bait bucket. I'll never see it again if I have to wait till Uncle Andrew gets the sheriff to search this place."

"And I say it probably isn't your bait bucket at all," Mart said. "Everyone around this lake has a bait bucket." He backed away from the window. "I think it's a good idea to go home. . . . There!" he added triumphantly as they went around the house. "You completely forgot what Linnie told you, didn't you, Trixie? She said she saw that wildcat's pelt nailed to this cabin, and there it is! Do you think someone who saved your life would be likely to steal from you and set fire to Mrs. Moore's cabin?"

Trixie hung her head. "I guess not, Mart, but I'm baffled. Say, nobody's even mentioned the Englishman. Linnie thought he lived here. I saw that dip net and bucket in his boat. Maybe *he* took my fish."

"There you go again, guessing," Brian said, shaking his head. "You're a dedicated flatfoot, all right. If the Englishman took your fish—and that's pretty improbable—then who set the fire? Who fired those shots in the woods just now?"

"There's only one person mean enough to fit the whole picture," Trixie answered.

"Right!" Mart said. "We'll be smart if we leave it to the sheriff from now on."

Back at the lodge all was still and dark.

"Thank goodness," Trixie said, "we didn't waken Mrs. Moore or Uncle Andrew. Listen! Listen!"

The katydids and frogs were quiet. In the hush, out on the lake below, they could hear the soft and regular splash of oars. The moon shone bright from a cloudless sky, and, as they all watched, a boat slid into its silver path, a lone figure at its oars.

Unexpected Meeting • 13

In spite of their expedition into the woods the night before, the Bob-Whites were up early. Trixie, Honey, Linnie, and Mrs. Moore were stirring around in the kitchen when Uncle Andrew came in.

"I guess you didn't rest any better than I did last night, did you?" he asked. "Most of the night I kept hearing queer noises. I imagined I heard someone moving about the house. I got up once and didn't see anyone and decided it was just my imagination. Did you hear anything?"

Trixie looked at Honey questioningly before answering him.

"Go ahead," Honey said. "We agreed before we came downstairs that we should tell Uncle Andrew all about last night. It doesn't matter, now that it's all over."

Uncle Andrew looked puzzled. "What are you talking about?"

So Trixie told him. The boys came into the kitchen while she was talking, looked sheepishly at one another, then interrupted her to add details she had forgotten.

"I told Mama, too," Linnie said. "She didn't like it."

Uncle Andrew's face was red. "I don't like it, either," he said emphatically. "I should have known that Trixie wouldn't rest until she went after that fish. I didn't think I'd have to sit up all night and watch. I guess I should be glad she didn't go alone. Trixie, you constantly keep me on pins and needles!"

"I'm sorry," Trixie said contritely. "I couldn't stand not knowing what happened to my fish."

"Now that you've been there, you don't know any more than you did before. I want to get to the bottom of the matter. I'm going to White Hole Springs to talk to Sam Owens. I suppose Slim is a hundred miles away from here by this time. He probably set the fire and skipped. The stranger you saw, man or spirit, doesn't sound to me like a criminal. The sheriff will throw some light on the matter."

"If Slim is gone, who fired that rifle?" Trixie asked.

"That's one of the things we must find out. When we do, we'll know whom you saw out on the lake at midnight last night, too. Are you planning to row across to that cave again today?"

"Oh, I *hope* so," Trixie said and looked expectantly at Jim and Brian. "I *know* we can find all the fish if we just get a chance to look for them without anything else happening."

"I wish you had a guide to go with you to replace Slim."

"I honestly think we know more about a cave than Slim does . . . Bob-White Cave, at least. Linnie said she'd go with us if her mother would give her permission. May she, please, Mrs. Moore?"

"I suppose so," Mrs. Moore said reluctantly. "I wish you'd just content yourselves with going fishing in Ghost River or the lake."

"With Slim gone, we'll get along just fine in the cave," Trixie urged.

"Do you think it'll be all right?" Mrs. Moore asked Uncle Andrew.

"If Linnie may go, yes. The Bob-Whites have proved themselves pretty reliable in the woods around their home in Sleepyside. Come back before five o'clock, and observe all the rules for spelunking!"

Over in the cave, in the big entrance room, Honey asked, "Do you have your lights? Three kinds for each one of you?"

They all checked and nodded.

"Do you have waterproof matches?"

Trixie held up the plastic envelope to show Honey. "How could we forget? Every time we come into the cave you check and double-check. Have we left a note outside? Have we brought our ropes? Do we have extra carbide for our lamps? Canteens? Chocolate bars?"

Honey looked dismayed. "I didn't know I was such a bossy person."

"Heavens, you aren't, Honey! We're as grateful as can be. At least, I am. I always get so excited about things that I never remember anything I should do. I couldn't accomplish anything without you, Honey."

"Well, now that the Admiration Society has concluded its meeting, shall we explore a little?" Mart asked. He led the way to the tunnel.

As they neared the wall, Trixie cried out, "Why, that's my bait bucket!"

"It is!" Honey said. "It's been right here all the time. That makes us look pretty foolish."

"It makes the bait bucket animated, if it's been here all the time. It didn't walk over here to the wall. I left it just inside the opening to the cave. Hurry; let's look inside!" Trixie threw back the lid and saw the ghost fish and crayfish.

"It *is* my bucket," she cried delightedly. "I wonder if Slim got scared and brought it back. Do you suppose it was Slim we saw on the lake last night? I've never known so many things to happen. I'm almost convinced that there *are* ghosts. I won't be separated from that bait bucket again. Here, Mart, see if you can push it ahead of you through the tunnel."

Mart led the procession. The crawlway was short, and they soon stood in the other room. They had forgotten how beautiful it was and turned their heads about, flashing their carbide lamps on the gleaming stalactites. "Mercy, what happened to them?" Honey cried. "They're broken off—dozens of them. Who'd do a thing like that?"

Apparently someone had taken a blunt instrument and deliberately knocked off the tips of many of the beautiful calcite formations.

"What a horrible thing to do!" Linnie said. "Some crazy person or somebody very evil did that."

"It was Slim," Trixie said positively. "No one else but us knew about this cave or this room. I hope Uncle Andrew gets the sheriff to find him."

"If it *was* Slim, it's sure strange about the bait bucket," Honey said. "He didn't have a change of heart and bring back the fish and then come on in here and wreck everything. I'm not too sure we should stay here. I think your uncle would want us to go right back to the lodge."

"There's no one here now. Please, Honey, let's look around and see if we can't find some more fish while we're right here on the spot," Trixie begged. "I just can't make any sense out of what's going on."

"*I* think Slim is in cahoots with that Englishman," Mart said. "*I* think they've been out here early this morning before we got here. *I* think they left the bait bucket here and didn't think we'd be over here today, after roaming the woods last night. *I* think it was Slim who shot that rifle last night, and *I* think he's working with that Mr. Glendenning."

"I'm *sure* it was Slim who fired the gun, but who was the man with the pack on his back? And what did he have in that pack? It wasn't the bait bucket," Trixie said.

Mart threw up his hands. "Let's forget the whole thing and work fast, before they get back. It was right over in this stream that Trix found the fish we do have."

Mart went down on his haunches and beamed his head lamp into the shallow water.

Trixie peered into the water, got up, went farther along the spring, and crouched again. "That's strange," she said. "I can see shadows on the bed of the stream, but I can't see anything in the water, can you?"

"They're the shadows of crayfish," Brian said. "They're transparent, like the one you have in the bucket. Though you can see right through them, the light doesn't go through very well, so a shadow is left. There aren't any fish here. Let's look farther along the stream."

Carefully they made their way around the hard flowstone, across wet clay, and over slippery rocks.

"It's the blackest black in this cave that I ever saw in my life," Honey said.

Mart laughed. "You can't *see* blackness."

"I wonder. Let's put out our lamps and find out how dark it would be."

"Not now!" Trixie said quickly. "Not when we're trying to find the fish!"

"Just for a little while," Honey said. "The rest of

us would like to try it. That is, I think so. Wouldn't you?"

"We'll never have a better chance," Brian said. "You can imagine you're a ghost fish, Trixie, and tell us where a bunch of spelunkers could find you."

Trixie laughed good-naturedly and put out her carbide lamp.

One by one, the others did the same.

The darkness was unbelievable. Not a person could see an inch in front of his face. It was eerie—and also frightening.

"Are we all here?" Honey asked breathlessly.

They laughed aloud to reassure themselves.

"Let's join hands," Linnie suggested. "Then we won't be so scared."

"Who's scared?" Mart asked, but he grasped Linnie's hand and held it hard. His voice echoed and re-echoed in the vaulted room.

Somewhere there was a rustling noise, as though a large animal had moved.

The drip-drip of the stalactites boomed as drops fell to waiting pools.

A fragment of limestone broke from the ceiling and dropped with what seemed a deafening crash.

A strange, weird sound came from inside the wall, a scratching sound, then a low moan!

"Was that someone groaning?" Trixie asked with a trembling voice.

A muffled sound answered her, unintelligible but unmistakably human.

147

"There's someone besides us in this cave!" Trixie cried and turned on her flashlight.

Other flashlights clicked, illuminating faintly the expanse of wall across the stream.

A deep, low moan came again, then the words "Get me out!"

"Hold it!" Jim answered. "We hear you."

Hurriedly the Bob-Whites lit their carbide lamps and gathered at the opening from which the voice came.

Trixie, more daring, her light leading her, crawled ahead into the tunnel. Not far from the opening, the passage narrowed sharply, and just ahead of her she saw blue-jeaned legs and the soles of shoes.

"Can you hold on a minute?" she asked.

"Get me out!" the voice cried.

Trixie backed. "There's a man stuck in there," she said. "Jim, you're the strongest. He'll have to be pulled out."

So Jim crawled in and tugged. The walls of the tunnel were slimy and wet. Jim pulled and pulled. Brian and Mart pulled at Jim's feet.

"He's easing out!" Jim cried. "Don't jerk my legs off. He's sliding on the wet clay. Get out of the way, Brian, Mart. Here we come!"

The boys inched back through the opening. Then Jim came out, covered with slimy yellow clay.

Then Slim!

The Bob-Whites' former guide was a sorry sight. His hands and face were masked over with clay through which blood oozed from raw scratches. He sat on the floor, gasping yet snarling, in spite of near exhaustion and suffocation.

"Wait till he gets his breath," Trixie said. "Then we'll soon find out what he's doing in Bob-White Cave."

Slim muttered angrily.

"And why he broke all the beautiful stalactites," Honey added indignantly.

"Let's give him a drink of water before we ask him anything," Trixie said. She opened her canteen and held it to him.

Slim slapped it to the ground. "Don't do me no favors!" he said. "Let me out of here!"

"That's enough of that!" Brian said disgustedly. "You're nothing but a stupid bully. You must have gone crazy to do all the damage you did around here."

"Yeah," Slim agreed slyly, "yeah . . . that's what it was. I dropped my candle. It went out. I went nuts in the darkness. I hammered around till I found that hole I got stuck in. You know how it is without any light. I heard you when you put your lights out. What would *you* do? Bust things up?"

"I hardly think so," Trixie said thoughtfully, "but I might go crazy and not know what I was doing. Why did you come here? Bob-White Cave is *our* cave. And why did you decide to bring back my bait bucket that you stole?"

"What bait bucket?" Slim asked, his dirt-encircled

149

eyes darting around. Then, when he saw the bucket with the ghost fish, he got up, cursed, and fiercely kicked it over. The ghost fish and crayfish slithered toward the stream, but Trixie was quick enough to recapture them and give them fresh water.

"That was a rotten, mean thing to do!" Jim said in a cold voice. "We *can* put you back in that crawl hole, fella. There are three of us."

"No, you won't!" Slim cried. "I'd die!"

"It's about time you realized that." Jim's voice was stern. He pointed. "That way out! Start walking!"

"And stay out of our cave!" Trixie added.

Slim stopped at the exit and said contemptuously, "Whose cave? This cave belongs to anyone who wants to explore it. It's state property."

"It's our cave," Trixie insisted. "It's on property that belongs to my Uncle Andrew. He said we could call it our cave."

"You'd better talk to the law," Slim said.

"You're a fine one to mention the law," Trixie said angrily. "You'll have some explaining to do to the sheriff about the fire that burned Mrs. Moore's property. If anyone had been—"

"I didn't set that fire!" Slim said. "There ain't nobody can prove I did. That guy in the ghost cabin did it. He ain't no ghost. He don't keep chickens in that chicken house of his'n. He keeps gasoline rags. If you don't believe me, go and look—lessen you're too scared," he added insolently. "I ain't afraid of you or the sheriff. I ain't afraid of nobody."

Slim started through the passage to the exit in the other room. "And I can come into this cave anytime I want to," he added. "When I signed up so's I could get the reward for the fish, I was told that I could try and find them in any cave around here. What do you think of that?"

"They meant if you had the owner's permission," Trixie said, "and you'll never get permission to explore Bob-White Cave."

"Who needs permission?" Slim asked sarcastically and disappeared into the short crawlway.

"Now I don't know what to believe," Mart said. "If there *are* gasoline rags at the ghost cabin, then—"

"I'd have to see them to believe Slim," Jim said. "We'll tell your Uncle Andrew, and the sheriff will look into it. After last night, I'm not in favor of any more amateur sleuthing."

"Well, *I* am," Trixie said, undaunted. "I'm not misled by Slim's talk about the gasoline rags. Did you happen to hear what he said about registering? Do you suppose we have to register before we can qualify for the reward?"

"It sure looks like it," Brian said. "If we'd had any sense, we'd have found out all the facts from that man from the magazine the last time we were in White Hole Springs."

Trixie picked up the bait bucket and threw the nylon rope over her shoulder. "It's just one more hurdle," she said resignedly. "If we have to register, we have to register. I just hope we're not too late."

Wild-Goose Chase • 14

AREN'T YOU BACK pretty early?" Uncle Andrew asked. "Did you get discouraged? Give up?"

"No!" they exploded in one voice. Then they told Uncle Andrew and Mrs. Moore what had happened.

"It's way past time that I talked to Sam Owens," Uncle Andrew said. "I guess I underestimated Slim's determination. I thought he'd be far away from here by now—scared of what the neighbors would do after that fire. Now he's trying to throw the blame on someone else. I'll have to go to town right away."

"May we go, too, so we can register?" Trixie asked.

"If Mrs. Moore says Linnie may take the mule wagon and drive us," Uncle Andrew said.

"Of course," Mrs. Moore said. "More than that, I'll

go along as far as the Hawkinses' cabin. Minnie Hawkins and I are piecing a quilt together."

"I just thought of something queer," Trixie said as they bounced along in the wagon behind Shem and Japheth. "Slim didn't know that bait bucket had been returned."

"No," Mart said slowly. "He didn't. That's odd."

"Did you hear what he said, Trixie, when he kicked the bait bucket over?" Honey asked.

"I just heard him snarl. Did he say something?"

"I'm almost sure I heard him say under his breath, 'That old coot!'"

"Yipe!" Mart yelled and almost fell out of the wagon. "The plot thickens."

As they drove past the ghost cabin, it looked deserted. "If we only had time, I wish we could stop here a minute," Trixie said. "I know Slim was lying about those gasoline rags in the shed over there, but I'd like to look around."

"We'll have to go as fast as the mules can go to get to White Hole Springs in time so I can see the sheriff," Uncle Andrew said.

"And so we can be sure to register," Honey reminded Trixie. "I've seen enough of that old haunted cabin to last a whole lifetime!"

"That's the way I feel, too," Linnie said, and she urged the mules on. "You remember Mama said it didn't pay to say you didn't believe in ghosts. Didn't you, Mama?"

"We have too many ghosts in these hills," Mrs. Moore said. "It's a pity that ghost cabin didn't burn down instead of my chicken house and cow shed."

"Even where we live, some of the old Dutch families believe in ghosts," Mart said. "They call them poltergeists."

"That's right," Trixie said. "They do. *I* never did. The Dutch people blame poltergeists when their cattle stray or a barn burns or they find their furniture broken up."

"When things like that happen in the Ozarks, we know it's the work of ghosts and witches," Mrs. Moore said. "I hope they've finished their evildoing now and will let us alone at the lodge. Here's the Hawkins place. I'll leave you. Their young people have gone berrying, so just their mother is at home."

She got out, and the wagon continued on its way.

In town they let Uncle Andrew out at the sheriff's office, then went to the motel where the editor was staying.

This time they went boldly to the desk and inquired for him.

"Right over there," the clerk said, pointing.

A dark-haired young man was scribbling away at a table. He raised his head as they approached.

"Are we too late?" Trixie asked breathlessly.

"Are you too late for what?" the young man inquired.

"To register for the reward," Trixie answered. "We've found one fish, and I'm sure we can find the

154

rest of them, if we aren't too late."

"You've found one?" the man asked, immediately interested. "A blind fish?"

"The partly blind one," Trixie explained. "But we'll get the others if there's time. We didn't know we had to register."

"You don't. What made you think you did?"

The Bob-Whites looked at one another. "That's another one of Slim's lies," Trixie whispered. "He wanted to get us out of the way this afternoon. Aren't we dummies to fall for anything he'd say?"

"I beg your pardon," the man said.

"Oh, nothing," Trixie said hastily. "Are there very many people trying to find the specimens?"

"I haven't any way of knowing," the editor told them. "Judging from the inquiries I've had, I'd say there may be a dozen or so."

Trixie's face fell. "Are there any rules we have to follow? All we know is what we read in your magazine article."

"That article said it all," the man answered. "I'll be greatly surprised if the *Scientific Digest* has a chance to pay the reward. The specimens we want are really pretty rare. You're the second person, though, to report finding a fish."

"Slim!" they chorused.

"He doesn't have it now," Trixie whispered. Out loud she asked, "Do you happen to know anyone named Sanderson?"

"No, I don't remember hearing that name."

"Oh, dear. May I ask you another question?"

"Fire away!"

Trixie never could understand why so many people found her earnestness amusing. "Do you know if there is any way of protecting our interests in a cave? I mean, if we find a place that seems to be exactly where the specimens can be found, can we have exclusive rights to it?"

"If the property belongs to you, or if you have the owner's permission to explore it, then you can have exclusive rights. I know of no other way."

Trixie's face brightened. "We *do* have the owner's permission to explore the cave where we found the fish. Does that mean you wouldn't consider fish from our cave unless *we* brought them to you?"

This time everyone laughed. "I'm afraid I'd have no way of recognizing fish from your cave," the man said. "In a country as wild as this seems to be, I guess you would just have to be prepared to defend your rights."

"That's exactly what we're going to do!" Trixie said. Then she said to Linnie and the Bob-Whites, "Just think what Slim may be doing, now that he's sent us on this wild-goose chase. Let's go and pick up Uncle Andrew and see what he's found out."

They said good-bye to the editor, then jumped into the wagon and drove over to the sheriff's office. Uncle Andrew was sitting inside talking to two men.

"Slim just wanted to get us out of the way," Trixie told him. "We didn't have to register at all."

156

"That's a shame," Uncle Andrew said. He left the men he was talking with and joined the Bob-Whites and Linnie. "The sheriff's out, but they think he'll be back soon. Here's a bundle of mail."

Trixie distributed the letters, then asked, "Do we have to wait till he comes back, Uncle Andrew?"

"I want to wait. That's the main reason I wanted to come to town. What's the big rush?"

"It's just that Slim tricked us so he could hunt around Bob-White Cave without anyone disturbing him. He knows just where we were hunting and just where we found the one ghost fish. We *have* to get back to the cave right away."

Uncle Andrew took out his watch. "When we get home, it'll be too late for any more cave hunting today. And don't get any ideas this time about slipping out at night, Trixie. I'll be prepared for that. Here's the sheriff now. Hi, Sam."

"Hi, Andy!"

The sheriff greeted Linnie and the Bob-Whites warmly. "Do you need any more pickaxes or ropes?" he asked. "Or a magnifying glass for the detectives? There, there, Trixie, don't turn up your pretty nose. I think you're quite a girl. What can I do for you now?"

"It's about Slim Sanderson," Uncle Andrew said and told the story of Slim's actions and of the suspicion that he had set the disastrous fire.

Mr. Owens sat awhile, stroking his chin. "That's a pretty serious charge, Andy," he said. "Slim's been up to quite a lot of mischief since his folks moved out, but nothing like setting fire to a widow's cabin. It'd take a low-down skunk to do that."

"We think that's a pretty good description of Slim," Uncle Andrew said. "I think the fire was meant to destroy the lodge as revenge on the young people and me for firing Slim as guide. Then the wind changed, and Mrs. Moore's buildings went up in flames instead."

"That's logical thinking," Sam Owens said. "But what puzzles me is that Slim was born and raised around here, and he knows what the penalty would be for setting any kind of fire."

"He swore he didn't do it. He said the old man who lives in the ghost cabin did it."

"That's an unlikely story. I met the man in the woods once and talked to him. He seemed to be harmless enough, just sort of bewildered."

"Slim said he's crazy and that there are some gasoline-soaked rags right now in a shed on his place."

"I can find out about that pretty quickly," the sheriff said. "I'll need to do some talking with both Slim and the man at the cabin."

"It's *not* a man," Linnie said positively. "It's a ghost. He floats through the air. I saw him. These people don't believe in spirits, Mr. Owens, but you do. The ghost cabin is haunted, and haunts have powers no live person has. You know that."

"Yes, Linnie, I do. I've also found that what's been laid to ghosts in the past has been done by a live person. Facts are what I'm after, and facts are what I'll have for you, Andy. Good day."

Even Shem and Japheth seemed dejected on the way back to the lodge. They plodded along stolidly, their eyes on the ground, their huge shoulders straining ahead of the swaying wagon.

The Bob-Whites were glad when they reached the Hawkinses' cabin and the children, browned and freckled, ran out. They hadn't long to visit, for Mrs. Moore turned to wave good-bye to her neighbor and, helped by Jim and Brian, stepped on the axle and into the wagon seat.

"You were later than I thought," she said. "It's a good thing I only have to warm up the dinner. What kept you?"

Uncle Andrew gave her a thumbnail sketch of their business in town.

"Minnie Hawkins couldn't believe what I told her about Slim's goings-on," Mrs. Moore said thoughtfully. "It appears to her and me that nobody's done anything about investigating that Englishman you fished out of the lake and that ghost at the cabin. She didn't have too good a word to say for Slim, but she thought if he was mixed up in the burning, the Englishman and the ghost were in on it, too."

As they neared the ghost cabin, Trixie said suddenly, "Can't we possibly stop for one minute and look in that shed?"

"Not that!" Mrs. Moore said quickly. "I don't want any more traffic with ghosts."

"It's broad daylight, and you can wait here in the wagon, you and Linnie and Uncle Andrew. We just

159

want to take one more look around . . . *please?* I have a feeling we should. Just for a minute."

"Then pull up, Linnie, please. We're late, but fifteen minutes more isn't going to make much difference. Just don't be longer than that, Trixie!"

"We won't. Thanks a million!" Trixie jumped down from the wagon and was halfway up the winding trail before the others started.

Mrs. Moore, in the wagon, covered her eyes and sat tapping her foot.

"Was your hunch right?" Uncle Andrew asked as the Bob-Whites came running back.

"I'll say it was!" Trixie said excitedly. "It looks as though Mrs. Hawkins was right. The culprits must be holing up in that ghost cabin. Just down the slope in back, we saw Mr. Glendenning digging away at the rocks with his pickax. He had a magnifying glass, and he kept examining the things he knocked off the cliff."

"That isn't any indication that he'd set a fire," Uncle Andrew said, his eyes twinkling.

"No, it isn't," Trixie agreed reluctantly. "But what we found later shows that he's what they call an accessory after the fact. We saw a gasoline can in the corner of the old shed near the house and, right next to it, a bundle of rags. I brought one along for evidence." Trixie tossed a dirty rag into the wagon next to Uncle Andrew.

"Phew! It's soaked with gasoline," Uncle Andrew said. "Well, that certainly is fire-starting material,

Trixie. I'll take it to Sam Owens."

"Does that let Slim out?" Honey asked.

"As far as the fire is concerned, maybe," Trixie said thoughtfully. "But he *did* steal our fish. I wish we had some way of keeping him out of Bob-White Cave."

"A way may turn up," Uncle Andrew said. "There's more to this whole business than meets the eye."

Sinkhole Suspense • 15

"Did anyone notice this note Moms tucked in with the letter we got in town yesterday? I didn't spot it till just now. Bad news."

Brian came into the living room, where the other Bob-Whites were assembling their gear, getting ready to go across the lake to the cave.

"I didn't see any note," Trixie answered, "just her letter. What is it?"

"She must have added it after she wrote the letter," Brian said. "We're going to have to go back home this coming Friday. And that's just three days from now."

"Heavens! Three days! We have a thousand things to do here. Why did Moms say we had to go home so soon?" Trixie took the sheet of paper from Brian and read it aloud.

"Your father just brought in the mail, and there was a letter from your Aunt Helen in Philadelphia. Uncle Mart has to go to the hospital for observation, and she wonders if I could come and stay with her. Of course I telephoned and told her I'd go. He is to go into the hospital next Monday, so I want to be there Saturday. That means I'll have to ask you to cut short your stay in Missouri. I'm sorry about this, but I know you will understand.

"If you can arrange to fly back from Springfield on Friday, Daddy and Bobby and I will meet the plane. I'm getting lonesome for all of you, and Bobby has been lost without you. When it is possible, send me a telegram to let me know when to expect you."

"That's terrible about Uncle Mart," Trixie said and folded the note. "I guess we really should go back as soon as we can."

"Friday will be all right, won't it, Trix, as Moms suggested?" Brian asked. "Your heart is set on collecting those specimens, and, gee . . . Jim and I did want to have a try for some rocks. What do you think, Uncle Andrew?"

"It'll be good for your Aunt Helen to have your mother with her. I think it's all right to follow her suggestion and leave for home Friday. I'll be sorry to have you go. I'd been planning a lot of things we could do as soon as Trixie had completed her project. Bill Hawkins was coming over today to help me with the shed for Shem and Japheth, but that can wait. If Linnie will drive me into town, I'll arrange for your

163

train tickets to Springfield, so you can connect with the plane for White Plains. I'll send a telegram to your parents, too, as soon as I know what flight you'll be on."

"Then let's get going!" Trixie said.

"Get going where?" her uncle asked.

"Across the lake to the cave, after the fish," Trixie said. "That is, if Slim didn't get ahead of us while he had us out of the way."

"Have you lost your mind, Trixie? Have you forgotten how mean that boy can be?"

"No, I haven't, Uncle Andrew, but what can Slim do, with Jim and Brian and Mart along?"

"I don't know what he can do, but I'm not going to take a chance. He'd stop at nothing to try for that reward. If I find that Sam Owens has him in custody, and if that man, ghost, or spirit at the ghost cabin is in jail, too, then I'll feel a lot different about further exploring."

"But, Uncle Andrew, please. . . ."

"No. Getting you all back home safe and sound is more important to me than any fish—"

"But it isn't more important to the kids!" Bill Hawkins had arrived and overheard the conversation. "If you have to go into town, Andy, I'll go over to the cave with the Bob-Whites."

Andrew Belden drew a long sigh of relief. "That's the answer, Bill," he said. "I did hate to disappoint Trixie again. I guess they all think I'm a pretty hard-boiled uncle."

"We do not; we think you're darling!" Trixie said. "And, oh, Mr. Hawkins, you're a lifesaver! Things will look a lot different, Uncle Andrew, when you get back from White Hole Springs. We'll have all those specimens down in Mrs. Moore's cold cellar in the galvanized tank you bought us."

"I just want to find you all safe and sound. I'm almost afraid to take my eyes off you."

"Don't worry, Andy," Bill Hawkins said. "There's only one way Slim could get to that cave, and that's by boat. I'll have my eye on that part of the lake every minute."

The Bob-Whites were all fond of Mr. Hawkins and delighted with the day's arrangement. When they arrived at the cave, however, Trixie had her first disappointment.

"Would you mind terribly," Jim asked, "if Brian and I went up on the cliffs over the cave and looked for rock specimens? The time's short, and we just might come up with some rocks that would be valuable. It isn't as though you didn't know exactly where to find the other ghost fish."

Trixie did wish Jim could hunt for the specimens with her. It would be so much more fun. She felt she mustn't be selfish, though, so she told the boys to go ahead.

"Say," Bill Hawkins interrupted, "I'm here to look after you kids. How can I do that if you're in half a dozen places? I can only be sure Slim doesn't sneak up on you if I keep my eye on the lake. Trixie can't go into that cave alone, even with Honey and Mart. If I go along with them, who's going to watch the lake?"

"Jim and I can watch it from up on the cliff," Brian said.

"Huh-uh; that won't do." Bill Hawkins shook his head. "I'll do the watching myself."

"There isn't any danger inside the cave; just two big rooms and the spring running through the second room," Brian said.

"Why don't you go into the cave with Trixie and see just what the setup is?" Jim said. "We'll watch right here while you do."

When Bill Hawkins emerged from the cave after his survey, he said, "I can't see a thing in there that'd harm three lively kids. I'll stay just outside the entrance, here, and watch the lake, too. Go ahead with your digging, boys."

So, one by one, Trixie, Mart, and Honey crept through the crawlway to the second room, pushing their buckets and knapsacks ahead of them.

"There's one thing we can be thankful for," Trixie said. "There's no sign that Slim was here while we were in town yesterday. That's a miracle. Something kept him away from here. Maybe he really did get scared about what the men would do to him for setting that fire."

"Yeah," Mart said. "He may be a long way from here by now."

"It's a break for us," Honey said. "What do you see in the stream, Trixie?"

166

"Nothing. Absolutely nothing!" Trixie said despairingly. She sat down on a jutting rock near the stream's edge and turned her flashlight on the wall nearest her. In the light she saw a pair of bright button eyes. A small pack rat looked timidly from a cleft in the rock. As Trixie watched, it ran out to the stream and along the water's edge, then disappeared.

"That's queer," she thought. "Where did it go?" She stood up to investigate and saw, across the stream, a deep grotto in the wall. Calling to Mart and Honey to follow, she stepped across and started walking ahead, her flashlight beaming at the ground ahead of her.

Suddenly she stopped, motionless with fright. A wide sinkhole yawned at her feet! Just one more step and she would have plunged down a dark hole.

"Don't come one inch nearer!" she warned. "I have to see where this leads. Lie down flat, then just creep up to the edge so we can look down."

Mart and Honey followed Trixie's lead, flattening themselves and crawling to the edge of the hole. When the light of their three carbide lamps shone down, they saw an amazing spectacle. Beneath the rim, the well widened like the inside of an inverted bucket, its sides a series of narrow ledges, slimy and dripping, descending about thirty feet and ending in a shimmer of water.

"It's awful!" Honey said. "You'd have fallen in just another second, and we'd never have seen you again. I can't look at it."

"I can," Mart said realistically. "There's nothing horrible about it except that it's blacker than night down there. Let's look around with our flashlights."

"Let's do!" Trixie said. "There, do you see what I see? The bottom of that hole is alive with ghost fish! And look at the salamanders crawling around the wall just above the water. Jeepers! It's a gold mine of ghosts!"

"We can't ever get them, either—unless—do you think we could tie a dip net on a rope and bring some of them up?" Honey asked. "Watch out, Trixie; don't go any nearer."

"There isn't anything to fear. Mart, salamanders can't possibly live in *deep* water, can they?" asked Trixie.

"Not on your life. Most of them don't live in water at all—just in damp places, usually."

"Then that means. . . ."

"Yeah! That there's only an inch or two of water at the bottom of that hole. Say. . . ."

"That's just what I'm thinking. One of us can easily go down there and get the fish—five hundred dollars' worth of fish!"

"Trixie Belden, I'll die if either one of you tries to go down into that awful place!" Honey cried. "I'll go and get Mr. Hawkins. Don't you *dare* to go down there!"

"I'd dare a lot more than that for five hundred dollars to put toward that station wagon. Why, Honey, I've gone down the side of a cliff on the Hudson River, a cliff lots higher than this well is deep, and you never said a word."

"It wasn't a black well, and it was a long way off from the river," Honey said, her voice quivering. "*Please*, Trixie, wait till tomorrow. We did promise your Uncle Andrew to obey all the cave rules."

"Did he mention anything about going down a little old well with water as shallow as this?"

"No, but we should wait and ask him or ask Mr. Hawkins, or go get Brian and Jim."

"And let all those fish get away? How do I know there isn't an outlet for that water so they'll vanish? Oh, Honey, it's just as safe as going down a cliff on the game preserve around your home. There are three of us in this cave together, aren't there? That's one of the main rules. Everybody knows we're inside this particular cave, don't they? That's another rule. We have plenty of light and good strong ropes, haven't we? Don't you see that it will be all right?"

"No, I don't. Why can't I at least get Jim and Brian, if you don't want me to tell Mr. Hawkins?"

"I don't want to wait, and they'd think we were sissies to call them away from rock hunting. There's just one thing, Mart. . . ."

"And that is?"

"I'll be the one to go down the rope."

Honey stifled a scream.

"Just why?" Mart asked.

"Because I weigh less," Trixie said.

"Even if you do, Mart couldn't possibly pull you

up. He couldn't even hold you when you'd be going down."

"Honey, did you ever hear of belaying? Watch. Mart, tie the end of the rope around this stalagmite, then around your waist. After running the other end around in back of you, I'll tie it around my waist. Now, brace your feet against that stone and sit back. See, Honey, what is there to be afraid of?"

"A million things. I just don't like it one bit."

Trixie squeezed her arm reassuringly. "Take another look, Honey. We can light up the whole inside of the well. See? Mart can run the rope around his waist when he's braced as he is now, and he can easily hold me. If he slips at all, I'll be holding on to a spare rope fastened to that stalagmite. See all those ledges that line the inside? It's easy as stepping down a ladder. Why, Honey, before you even know it, I'll be down there and sending up a bucket of ghost fish."

Honey just stood and watched, wringing her hands.

Mart put himself in the proper position at the edge of the hole and let down the spare rope. Then Trixie grasped the belay rope, wrapped the end of it firmly about her waist, and knotted it. "See, Honey, we've fastened the ropes, Mart and I, just the way mountain climbers do!" she said, and she fastened her flashlight to her belt, pushed the dip net through a loop, and slipped the bail of the bucket over her arm.

Then, her gloved hands grasping the spare rope, she grinned encouragingly at Honey and stepped back over the rim to the first ledge, a knee's length below.

Lower and lower Trixie went, with Mart letting out the rope. She mustn't look up. That was against cave rules, for even a small bit of sand could get into her eyes. So she kept her head turned down, her carbide lamp lighting the way ahead of her, and, the rope firm above her, went from step to step, lower, lower, lower, till she stood in shallow water at the bottom of the sinkhole.

The floor was swarming with small, round, white worms, the food the man from the magazine said was best for the fish. Without looking up she called to Mart, "I'll send up a bucket of worms first." Her voice echoed and reechoed, booming from wall to wall till it escaped at the rim.

Mart called something back, but the sound disintegrated so that Trixie couldn't understand a word. She filled the bucket, gave two short jerks to the spare rope, and felt the bucket start to lift.

Tiny ghost fish, alarmed at the motion of her net in the water, darted frantically out of sight. On the other side more swam into view. "This water runs right through the bottom of this hole," Trixie thought, bringing the fish in with the net.

The empty bucket came down on the rope and plopped into the water beside Trixie. She waited, watched, then dip, splash—eureka! Two small fish went into her bucket. She got a crayfish, then another, and all the while she watched for more fish.

Close to where she was standing, a yellowish lizard-like creature crept, its blob of a head too big for its body, and its legs almost too weak to hold its weight. Trixie popped it into the bucket, jerked her signal to Mart, and the bucket moved up.

"I hope I can send up more fish next time," she thought and looked intently into the shallow water. Fish, worms, everything had disappeared!

"What can have happened?" she thought—then became terrified. Water was creeping higher on her boots. It was running in from some hidden source—rising!

"I have to get out of here!" Trixie thought. She was aware at the same moment of Mart's voice, and the shrill voice of Honey. "They're warning me!" she thought as the belay rope slapped against her waist and the spare rope twirled back down. "They're scared, too."

"I'm coming!" she called up. "Pull, Mart! Pull! I'm coming! I'm coming right now."

The water had nearly reached the top of her boots as she held the rope taut and began to climb up.

What had seemed so easy in descent became a nightmare. Small ledges that had held her corrugated soles so easily on the way down escaped her feet as she sought anchorage. The trickle of water that had dripped over the brim as she started down became a cascade, dousing her carbide lamp as her feet slipped from any hold, and she swung free in the cold, inky darkness.

"Mart!" she called frantically.

If any answer came, it was drowned in the roar of

the waterfall that threatened to drown her from above.

Prayerfully, Trixie held on. She managed to loop the spare rope about her right hand, and she held on with all her strength. Her body hung like a pendulum as she swung from side to side. Terrified, she reached for a foothold, gained it, then lost it to swing again under the choking rush of icy water.

Slowly, oh, so very slowly, it seemed she was being raised. Or did she only imagine it? Now cold water from below crept up her body as high as her waist.

Suddenly the upward pull stopped. Her arms holding the rope slackened. "I just *can't* hold on any longer," Trixie thought. "Oh, Moms! Daddy! Someone help me!"

Lessons to Learn · 16

THE NOISE around Trixie grew louder and louder. Water splashed from above, gurgled from below, menacing, nearing. *Voices ... voices. ...* Mart shouted something. Honey screamed. *Voices ... voices ... the rope isn't moving up. ... Mart's drowned. ... Honey's drowned. ... This awful ... awful water.*

In her confusion, Trixie imagined she saw white shapes moving about her, clouds of white shapes, ghosts of people, ghosts of fish ... ghosts ... ghosts.

Doggedly she held on; in frenzied desperation, she reached for a toehold, anything to propel herself upward from the swirling water, which was now up to her armpits.

That ghostly light ... voices nearer ... then a

174

vigorous sharp tug at the rope! The ghostly forms merged into a blur of head lamps. Strong arms reached for Trixie, pulled her over the edge of the sinkhole, and gathered her up.

With a great sigh, Trixie opened her eyes and looked into Jim's anxious blue eyes. Quietness came. "I'm safe," she thought, "safe."

Water covered even the floor of the entrance room as Jim carried Trixie outside and placed her on a pallet Honey had made of their sweat shirts. Then they all waited, watching carefully while she rested.

The sun burst through the curtain of black clouds that had brought the cloudburst to swell the underground spring.

"That rain was a hazard nobody thought of," Jim whispered.

"There we were, sheltered under the ledge, till Honey shouted for us," Brian said in a low voice.

"In the minute it took me to get inside, she could have drowned," Bill Hawkins said. "What a guardian I turned out to be!"

Honey said nothing but "Poor Trixie! Poor Trixie!" over and over again, till the refrain sparked Trixie's sense of humor, and she sat up, laughing.

"You look like Chinese professional mourners," she said. "I'm all right. I'm a little damp, but I'm all right!" She stretched her arms, pretending to feel her muscles. "What happened?"

"What a girl!" Jim said. Then he told Trixie of the quick thunderstorm that had come up unexpectedly,

175

just as it had the day after they arrived at the lodge. "It seemed as though the whole lake fell on us."

"We never dreamed you'd be in danger in the cave," Brian said. "In fact, we remarked that it was fortunate you were under cover."

"We took cover under the ledge to wait out the storm," Jim said. "Suddenly there was Honey, struggling through the downpour, calling for help."

"We ran to help, and then everything happened at once," Brian went on. "There was Mr. Hawkins, flat on his face, trying to bring you up. And there was Mart, practically purple, holding on to the rope, the water gushing in, the stream roaring, a waterfall as big as Niagara pouring over the edge of a big hole, and Honey screaming that Trixie was down there!"

"We don't know what happened from then on," Jim said. "We only know that we brought you up in time—thank God, in time!"

"Did you save my fish?" Trixie asked.

Her question, so anticlimactic, brought a burst of relieved laughter.

"The fish and other stuff are in the bucket," Mart said, "and their delicious food in this other bucket." He tipped the bait pail so Trixie could see the squirming worms.

"Oh, down at the bottom there are hundreds of ghost fish," Trixie said. "Did I get *any* of them, Mart? I don't seem to remember right now."

"Two ghost fish, a salamander, two white crayfish, and a bunch of round ghost worms," Mart recited.

"And a partridge in a pear tree!" Trixie mimicked. "But two fish are not enough. After that awful trip after them, we still don't have specimens that'll win the reward. Brian! Jim!" Trixie looked expectantly toward the cave. "I'll bet that water's gone down, now that the rain's stopped."

"Good grief, Trixie! Go down that hole again? Not for a million miserable ghost fish!" Mart threw his hands over his head and made a gesture of complete bewilderment.

"I didn't mean go down right now," Trixie said.

"Well, I mean *never* go down again, no matter what we'd find at the bottom. One experience like that will last me!" Mart was emphatic.

"I don't even want to come over on this side of the lake again," Honey said, her voice quivering.

Bill Hawkins, still dazed, just kept repeating, "It was all my fault—all my fault."

"It wasn't anyone's fault except my very own," Trixie said.

"Say what you want, I was responsible. If it had been one of my own children down there, I couldn't feel worse. All I thought about was keeping a lookout for Slim. I even saw the clouds and knew it was going to rain. It never occurred to me there'd be any danger from rain *inside* the cave."

"It's all over now, and that's all we need to care about," Trixie said. "Except, gosh, I wish Uncle Andrew didn't have to know I went down in that sinkhole like that."

"Or that I let you go," Mart said.

"And me," Honey added.

"He'll have a good right never to speak to me again," Bill Hawkins said. "Let's go over to the lodge now. Trixie needs dry clothes and something hot to drink. We might as well face Andy Belden now as later."

"You're all soaked through," Mrs. Moore said as they trooped into the lodge. "I could see that downpour across the lake. It hardly rained here at all. My! You look almost drowned!"

Honey caught her breath at the word, but Trixie said quickly, "We did get pretty wet. I guess we'd better change our clothes."

"I'll make some hot chocolate," Mrs. Moore said. "Bill, will you have some coffee, or are you in too much of a hurry to go on home?"

"I'm not going home till I get a chance to talk to Andy," Hawkins said. "I'll have a cup of coffee, please, then I'll go out and work on the mule shed till he gets here."

"Everybody acts so queer," Mrs. Moore said to the Bob-Whites after they'd changed to dry clothes. "Bill hardly drank a spoonful of coffee. Did anything happen over there in the cave? Was that Slim up to more of his wickedness?"

"Jim, bring out the bait buckets, please, and show Mrs. Moore what we found today," Trixie said as she sipped her hot chocolate. "We found fish and salamanders, and Mart has a queer beetle and a spider in his specimen jar. It was quite a day!"

"You can say that again!" Mart said solemnly.

Jim showed Mrs. Moore the fish, then he and the other boys took the buckets down to the cold cellar to the galvanized tank.

"You aren't fooling me one bit, Trixie Belden," Mrs. Moore said when they had gone. "I know something out of the way happened at the cave. Look at Honey's face!"

"My face?" Honey asked. "What's wrong with my face?"

"It has fright printed all over it," Mrs. Moore said. "I don't have a daughter your age without being able to read a girl's face. Never mind; your uncle and Linnie just drove in the yard, and it won't take him long to find out what's wrong."

It *didn't* take Uncle Andrew long to find out, because Bill Hawkins told him as soon as he stepped from the wagon. The Bob-Whites saw him in earnest conversation with Uncle Andrew and ran out into the yard. Mrs. Moore followed.

Trixie put her arms around her uncle. He held her close to him and listened, white-faced, till Bill Hawkins finished his story.

"It wasn't that way at all," Trixie tried to explain. "It wasn't Mr. Hawkins's fault. It was every single bit mine, no matter what anyone says."

Uncle Andrew's arms tightened around Trixie. "My own brother's child nearly drowned. Oh, I do thank

God you're safe. These children," he said to Bill Hawkins, "are as dear to me as they could possibly be if they were my own. To think how near we came to losing this little girl! How could you, Bill?"

Mrs. Moore held her apron over her face and cried unrestrainedly.

"It *wasn't* Mr. Hawkins's fault. I keep telling you that, Uncle Andrew. He didn't know a thing about what was going on inside that cave. He was watching for Slim outside, just as you told him to. Tell him you don't blame him, please. He feels so bad!"

"It'll take me some time to do that, Trixie. I'm sorry, Bill, but that's the way it has to be."

"I don't blame you a bit, Andy. It'll be a longer time till I forgive myself. I've still got to tell Minnie about it, too." He strode off up the trail that led to his house.

"I hate to see him so worried. He's such a nice man, and, jeepers, Uncle Andrew, I'm all right. Don't think I wasn't scared, because I was, but, heavens, I don't want everyone to get so worked up about it. The Bob-Whites rallied to help. They always do. *Nothing* can happen to one of us when the others are near . . . *nothing!*"

"I wish I were as convinced of that as you are, Trixie. The Bob-Whites are a fine group of young people. No doubt about that. But remember this!" He shook his finger to emphasize his statement. "No more spelunking for any of you! I want to see you get on that train to Springfield in one piece. I don't expect more than *one* miracle to happen in a few days' time. I've been blessed with two. Trixie was saved from that wildcat, and now she's been saved from drowning. I don't intend to try the mercy of the Almighty too far." Uncle Andrew's voice shook with vehemence born of released tension.

Amazed and shocked at her uncle's mandate, Trixie took some time to find her voice.

"You can't possibly mean that! That cave is just full of ghost fish! We *have* to earn that reward. We *have* to have the five hundred dollars!"

"I'll give you five hundred gladly," Uncle Andrew said.

Trixie shook her head positively. "We can't take it from you. We've never had one penny given to us for one of our projects. We've always *earned* the money. Oh, dear, I just *know* we can find all three specimens that man wants! Uncle Andrew, *please!*"

"Not one step into any cave," Uncle Andrew said, his face grim. "What a day!" He straightened and seemed to pull himself together with an effort. "Mrs. Moore, I think we'll all feel better when we've had our dinner."

Dinner didn't help. No one could eat. No one could say a word. Once, in the living room after dinner, Jim tried to change Uncle Andrew's mind. "We could take some solid beams and lay them across that hole. With a rope ladder fastened to them, it would be a breeze to go down in that well," he began.

Uncle Andrew just held up his hand, and Jim was

silenced. "We've had enough of that subject. Even though you haven't asked me, I'll tell you about my talk with Sam Owens today."

"It went out of my mind completely," Trixie said. "Did he question Slim?"

"He couldn't find him. Somebody told Sam they thought they saw Slim getting into a boxcar as the morning freight pulled out of White Hole Springs."

"Doesn't that look as though he's guilty?" Mart asked.

"It does. The men I saw in town were stirred up over the rumor that he set the fire. He may have been afraid of a necktie party."

"Did Mr. Owens question the man in the ghost cabin?"

"He couldn't find him, either. He disappeared into the woods. But I talked with Mr. Glendenning, the Englishman you Bob-Whites saved from the lake. He stayed for a while at the ghost cabin, you'll recall."

"What did he say?" Trixie asked eagerly.

"That the man he stayed with wouldn't hurt a fly. He said he was sort of confused—maybe a little off in the head—but the kindest person he ever knew."

"With those gasoline rags in his shed and the gasoline can there, too?" Mart asked.

"Mr. Glendenning said the rags and can belonged to him. It wasn't gasoline. It just smelled like it. It was carbon tetrachloride, and he used it for cleaning the rock specimens he dug out of the hillside."

"There goes Slim's defense. That and the fact that

he ran away. Couldn't the sheriff have sent word ahead to the next station by telegraph to have Slim picked up there?"

"He did that. Either Slim was good at hiding, or the man never saw him get on the freight in the first place. He wasn't on it when the officer at Laurel, the next stop, searched the train. Mr. Glendenning said something else," Uncle Andrew went on. "He said that when Slim rowed his boat back for him the day you Bob-Whites rescued him, Slim told him he knew where the ghost fish specimens could be found and he'd show him for a price. Mr. Glendenning didn't see anything wrong with that, and one evening Slim took him over to the cave."

"He showed him our fish," Trixie said breathlessly.

"He did. Mr. Glendenning said he recognized it as a ghost fish, paid Slim a good price for it, and took it to the cabin in the bait bucket it was in. Then, while he was in town, the bait bucket disappeared. He has no idea how it got back to the cave. Anyway—" Uncle Andrew drew a deep breath—"I've a feeling we've seen the last of a young scoundrel named Slim. White Hole Springs or anyplace else around here would be too hot for him to set foot in."

"I don't know what makes people bad the way Slim is," Honey said. "Maybe if he'd ever had a chance...."

"I gave him a chance when I hired him to act as your guide. He just didn't recognize it. Till the day he dies, he'll think it's easier to make a dollar by stealing than by hard work. When blame is being passed

183

around, I surely can claim my share for ever letting him in the same room with you young people. It's a lesson to me. The fact is, we've all learned a lot, and it's time we turned in and thought it over."

Misplaced Memory · 17

AFTER THEY WENT upstairs, the Bob-Whites had a conference in the girls' room. They sat around with glum faces.

"I know just what you're all thinking," Trixie said. "You're thinking that if I hadn't gone down into that sinkhole in the cave, we wouldn't be confined to quarters. You're right. But, jeepers, we wouldn't have any fish, either."

"If you'd sent up more ghost fish in that bucket instead of the darned old worms," Mart said, "we'd probably be sitting on Cloud Nine, with the reward in our hands."

"I'm so glad Trixie is safe that I don't want to blame anyone," Honey said. "If we don't find any more ghost fish, we'll think up some other way of raising money after we go back home. We've always been able to find a way when we needed to. Maybe we could have a talent show or some sort of sale. . . ."

Trixie got up from her seat on the side of the bed, took her mother's letter from the dresser, read it, folded it, and turned around to the group.

"Have we ever in our lives started a project and not finished it? No. Then are we going to leave this project unfinished if it's humanly possible not to? No. Let's go downstairs right now and talk it out with Uncle Andrew. *Of course* I was foolish to go down in that well, but how did I know a cloudburst was on its way? I'd have been perfectly safe if that hadn't happened."

"That's debatable," Jim said. "You should have told Bill Hawkins, and you should have called Brian and me, but you know that now, and I'm not going to say any more. Right now, if you think my opinion is worth anything, I feel it would be a mistake to go downstairs and talk to your uncle again tonight. He's had a terrible shock. I think our chances are better if we talk to him tomorrow."

"I heartily agree," Brian said. "If we can come up with some idea that will insure a maximum of safety, he may change his mind. Gosh, I can't keep my eyes open any longer. Let's all hit the sack. Good night, Trix, Honey."

The boys went to their room, and the lodge darkened for the night.

The next morning it didn't seem as though Brian was a very good prophet.

The Bob-Whites visited the tank in the cold cellar room and came back with long faces. An inventory had shown two ghost fish in the middle stage of evolution and one with eyes, but none wholly eyeless. That meant the evolutionary sequence was not complete, and they couldn't possibly qualify for the reward. The ghost salamander was extra and probably had no value; neither did the crayfish or the other specimens Mart had. Brian and Jim's rock specimens shone bright with minerals when they put them under a light, but they were only souvenirs.

Uncle Andrew was affable. He laughed and talked about many things—but not about ghost fish and the reward.

The Bob-Whites were subdued and quiet. They were polite, but they couldn't think of anything to say.

Uncle Andrew seemed to be able to take just so much of their silence and gloomy faces; then he exploded.

"All right, out with it. I can't stand having all of you act like chief mourners. Even Jacob acts as if I'm an unfriendly stranger."

Trixie started to speak.

Uncle Andrew held up his hand. "Never mind. I know what's bothering you. It's that blasted fish. I haven't changed my mind one bit about the danger you'd be getting into, but—"

Trixie jumped from her seat.

"But something Jim said last night stayed in my mind. He spoke of putting strong beams across the top of the hole and—"

"We *could* do it, Uncle Andrew!" Trixie clapped her hands and shouted. "There are beams right outside in the lumber pile. Hooray!"

"Not so fast, young lady. If there's to be another expedition to the cave, *I'll* go, too."

"That would be great!" Mart said.

"You can see for yourself, then, that there's no danger when it isn't raining," Trixie said. "May we start?"

"In a little while," Uncle Andrew said.

"We only have today. Tomorrow we have to take the specimens to the man in White Hole Springs and then leave for home. *Please*, Uncle Andrew?" Trixie pleaded.

"I want to wait for one thing; then we can start," Uncle Andrew said. "Linnie, please ride over and ask Bill Hawkins if he'd join us. Tell him I need him."

Trixie ran to her uncle and hugged him. "You're an old fraud and a darling!" she said. "Mr. Hawkins will be so relieved to have you say that. I felt sorry for him last night."

"Try feeling sorry for me, with my responsibility," Uncle Andrew said. "And, for heaven's sake, stay close to Bill and me, all of you, and be careful!"

When they entered the cave, they found that the water had receded, leaving the clay floor slippery and mottled with pools. With some difficulty they shoved wooden beams through the crawlway to the room where the sinkhole was.

"If there's still deep water in that hole, I'll just die!" Trixie said under her breath to Jim. "We'll never get Uncle Andrew to come over here again."

Carefully they made their way across the room, around the stalagmites and rocks, to the edge of the sinkhole. Inside, happily, the water had drained to the level at which it had been when Trixie went down the day before.

Uncle Andrew and Bill Hawkins circled the hole and bent frequently to look down into its depths.

"See!" Trixie said. "There's nothing to be afraid of."

"You're irrepressible, Trixie," her uncle said.

"I have another word for it," Mart said. "Let me be the one to go down this time. I weigh less than Jim or Brian."

"No—please, please, no!" Trixie protested. "*I* want to be the one to go. I was down there once, and I know just what to do. *Please!*"

"It's no place for a girl," Uncle Andrew answered quickly. "You almost died down there yesterday, Trixie. Do you want to take another chance?"

"Yes, yes, I do. It's only right. I saw the fish, and I want to be the one to go after them. Mr. Hawkins, tell Uncle Andrew there's no danger now. It was that cloudburst that was to blame."

"I'm not the one to say," Bill Hawkins answered.

189

"She's a spunky young 'un, I will say that."

"There'll be *six* of us up here to watch," Jim said. "Her heart's so set on being the one to get the fish. You might as well let her go, Mr. Belden."

Reluctantly Uncle Andrew gave his consent. He watched intently while Jim and Brian carefully placed the beams over the hole and securely adjusted the rope ladder.

"This will be a breeze this time," Trixie said exultantly and went down the ladder.

The rain had washed in an assortment of queer creatures—transparent crayfish, flatworms, spiders, beetles, and salamanders.

"Don't waste any time on worms," Mart called. "Do you see any fish?"

"Swarms of them!" Trixie called up triumphantly. She dipped her net again and again and sent the plastic bucket to the top.

"Are they the right kind?" she called.

"There's another one with eyes," Jim answered.

"And more with just bumps for eyes . . . two of them, I mean," Brian added.

"And some . . . yes, two with no eyes at all!" Honey cried.

"That's all you're after, isn't it?" Uncle Andrew, kneeling, asked anxiously, his huge flashlight illuminating the whole inside of the hole.

"Send up a few more for good luck!" Mart shouted. "Then come on up, Trixie."

Trixie did as Mart asked. Then, holding tight to the

ladder, she carefully climbed to the top and out. Her clothes were soaked, but she didn't care. "Just look at them!" she shouted. "Right there in those bait buckets! Aren't they beautiful?"

"Five hundred dollars' worth," Mart said, then added, "I hope."

Trixie whirled around. "What do you mean, you hope?" she asked.

"Someone could have found the specimens ahead of us."

"What a horrible thought, Mart Belden! I've had the strangest feeling ever since we've been here, though, that Slim is around someplace."

"Stop bothering about Slim," Jim said and picked up one of the bait buckets. "I think you struck gold in this cave. I doubt whether there's another spot like it."

"Well, then," Trixie said confidently, "we'll just get them into White Hole Springs and settle the whole business. Isn't it wonderful?"

Uncle Andrew watched, relieved, as the Bob-Whites assembled all their paraphernalia and crept back through the crawlway. "Now that's over, I can rest peacefully for a while," he said.

He spoke too soon.

When they emerged from the cave, an appalling thing was happening down on the beach, right in front of their eyes.

"It's Slim!" Trixie screamed. "Hurry! He's killing a man! Jim!"

Slim, immediately aware that he had been seen, quickly pushed the man to the ground and dashed toward his boat.

Jim, swift as a deer, attacked with a flying lunge. Slim dodged adroitly and delivered a swinging right that struck Jim on the jaw and threw him to his hands and knees. Slim backed off then and edged toward the waiting boat, grinning insolently.

Brian started to Jim's assistance, but Uncle Andrew waved him back. "Jim can take him! He doesn't want help."

With that, Jim was up again, crouching and weaving, closing in on Slim. This time he landed a hard one-two that caught Slim off guard and took his wind. In a second Jim was at him, his right shoulder lowered. Before Slim knew what had happened, he went cartwheeling over Jim's shoulder and fell, spread-eagled, on the ground.

"Tie him up now!" Jim called, dusting his hands.

Elated, Brian and Mart quickly bound Slim with their nylon ropes. He lay inert, panting and cursing.

"That stunt, with all the rest of your meanness, will get you a good term in the pokey," Bill Hawkins said sternly. He picked up the rifle that lay close to the water's edge.

"A killer," Uncle Andrew said soberly. "That's the kind of guide I picked for these young people. I'd like to be on the jury that tries him."

"It ain't my gun," Slim mumbled. "It's his'n." He jerked his head toward his victim.

Swiftly Trixie and Honey turned their attention to the fallen man. Half-conscious, he put his hand again and again to his head. He groaned pitifully.

"Get some water, please, Mart," Trixie said. "Cold water from the spring inside the cave. I'll make a compress." She pulled her scarf from her neck, dipped it into the water Mart brought, and folded it across the man's forehead. He relaxed at once, visibly relieved.

"Let Brian examine him," Honey said. "He's going to be a doctor," she explained proudly to Bill Hawkins.

"There aren't any broken bones," Brian said. "It's mostly his head that's hurt. Trixie, you and Honey keep changing that compress. There—see—he's opening his eyes."

Bill Hawkins drew a quick breath. "It's the stranger from the ghost cabin! With all those blond whiskers, no wonder everyone took him for a white-haired ghost. He's coming to now, isn't he?"

Weakly the man raised his hand, brushed it across his eyes as though to clear his vision, attempted to sit up, blinked at the girls, then shook his head sadly. "No," he said to himself, "it's not either of them."

"Take it easy, sir," Brian warned. "You've been badly hurt!"

"My head!" the man said. "Where am I? Where's Slim?"

"You're with friends," Uncle Andrew assured him. "We'll take care of you as soon as you feel a little stronger. As for Slim, he's trussed up down there on the beach, waiting for the sheriff."

"He had no right to jump on me," the man said. "I was only trying to help the young people."

The Bob-Whites looked at one another, puzzled.

"Where am I?" the man asked again, blinking in bewilderment.

"Outside a cave on the shore of Lake Wamatosa," Uncle Andrew said. "Don't worry about it now. Save your strength."

"Lake Wamatosa!" the man repeated, his blue eyes full of wonder. "Lake Wamatosa! . . . I remember it! Did you hear what I said? I *remember* it!"

"It's like I thought," Bill Hawkins said in a low voice as his forefinger traced a circle at his forehead. "He's crazy."

"I don't think so," Uncle Andrew said. "I don't think so at all. Are you feeling stronger?" he asked the man.

"I can walk all right," the man said and raised himself. He shook his head dizzily, then got to his feet. "If you will just get me across to the other side, there's someone there I've got to find."

"We'll take you," Jim said, and he and Brian put the man's arms across their shoulders and half led, half carried him down to the boat.

Bill Hawkins quickly checked the ropes trussing Slim, then joined the others. "I'll go along, just in case," he said. "That one'll keep until I come back for him."

"What did that man mean about helping us?" Trixie asked Honey. "I don't understand."

"I don't know. Too many things are happening. I'm

so bewildered I don't know what to think."

"Me, too," Trixie said. "It's a real mystery."

It was a little harder to get the stranger up the winding path from the lake to the lodge.

"That isn't the path!" he kept protesting. "Now, if you'll just let me find the way myself. . . . This is not the path!"

Uncle Andrew, Bill Hawkins, and the boys persisted, however. They wanted Mrs. Moore to bandage the man's head and give him a hot drink.

"This path leads to my lodge," Uncle Andrew said. "You can rest there. It's at the top of this cliff. When you feel better, you may go on by yourself."

"I don't know this path," the man muttered. "I'm not sure I know you. But you're mighty kind, stranger, mighty kind." His voice weakened, and his body sagged. "I guess I could take a little help, boys."

He collapsed, and the boys carried him the rest of the way to the lodge, up the steps, and into the big living room, where they lowered him to the couch. "I'm sorry," he said weakly. "I thought I could make it. . . . I've got to keep going . . . so close now . . . so close. . . ."

"Now," Bill Hawkins said, "I'll get Slim and dump him into the mule wagon. If you'll lend me the mules, I'll turn him over to Sam Owens."

Mrs. Moore and Linnie had been working in their own cabin, but when they heard the Bob-Whites' voices, they hurried over to the lodge.

Uncle Andrew met them at the door. "A man's been hurt," he told Mrs. Moore. "We need your help."

Mrs. Moore hurried anxiously to the couch and bent over the injured man. His eyes were closed. "Is he badly hurt?" she inquired. "How did it happen?"

At her voice, the man's blue eyes opened wide. "Annie!" he cried. "My Annie!"

"God in Heaven!" Mrs. Moore cried, down on her knees, her face close to the stranger's. "Is it Matthew? Back from the dead? Is it his ghost?" She ran her hand over the cloud of blond hair and whiskers. "Oh, Matthew, speak to me! What happened? Are you alive? Mr. Belden, where was he? Is he man or ghost?"

"He's alive, Mrs. Moore," Uncle Andrew said gently, hardly able, himself, to speak.

"Is it really your father?" Trixie asked, her voice filled with awe. "Linnie, can it be your very own father, alive?"

"If Mama says so," Linnie said, her voice trembling. "If she knows him, then it's my daddy!" She dropped on her knees and put her arm across her father. "Oh, Daddy," she cried, tears streaming, "we needed you so!"

"Well, I'll be a monkey's brother-in-law's aunt's sister," said Mart and broke the tension. "Jeepers creepers, do things ever happen to us! He's been living in the old ghost cabin a short way from here. Why didn't he let his family know?"

"I think something happened, and he lost his memory," Brian said thoughtfully. "It does happen. When

196

his head was battered by Slim, his memory must have returned."

"I think you're right," Jim agreed. "Gee, I'm sure glad for Mrs. Moore and Linnie."

"And how!" Mart said. "I'll bet the first thing he'll want is a shave. That blond halo fooled a lot of people. He made a number-one ghost. And, say, he's been up to some queer tricks . . . that bundle over his shoulder, those gunshots, all that wandering around he's done, scaring people. Gosh, look at Jacob, licking his hand."

"Yes, that's one of the things that seemed strange about the ghost," Trixie said, "the way Jacob followed him and never barked at him."

"I always told you horses and dogs know a lot more than people think they do," Honey said. "Isn't it all just wonderful?"

"He still has a few things to clear up," Mart said skeptically.

When Matthew Moore had rested and was stronger, he cleared up quite a few things.

"I was hunting over near Wagon Trail, south of Springfield," he said. "You know, Annie, that wild country where I liked best to go. One day I ran into a man—a bad man, a very bad man—in the woods. He wanted me to give him money. You know, Annie, I never had much money; just fished, slept outdoors, and camped. He grabbed my knapsack when he found I hadn't any money, and he jumped on me and tried to kill me. He tried to shove me off the cliff where we were. I struggled with him, and we both went over. I hit a ledge; then I guess I blacked out. He went on down, over the cliff."

"Then it must have been *his* body they found," Mrs. Moore said, her voice low. "He had your knapsack. They sent it to me, Matthew."

"And you thought I was dead? Oh, Annie! I was worse than dead. I've been worse than dead for all these years. Linnie was only four. . . ." His voice quivered, and he held his daughter's hand tight.

"Where *have* you been all these years?" Mrs. Moore asked, her voice filled with concern. "Have you been sick, Matthew?"

"Some men who were surveying found me on the ledge where I fell. They took me to Springfield, and no one there knew who I was. I couldn't tell them. I was in a hospital. They gave me good care, but they couldn't bring my mind back. When I was strong again, I worked around the hospital grounds. I saved the money they paid me. I've got a good bit, Annie. No one robbed me. I'll get it for you."

"Didn't you remember me or Linnie?" Mrs. Moore asked.

"In the back of my mind I did. There was something that bothered me all the time. When I'd see a young girl, I'd try so hard to remember. I must have been thinking of Linnie. That's why I was so glad I shot that wildcat. I thought every young girl I saw might be mine."

"Then it was *you* who saved my life!" Trixie cried. "Oh, thank you, Mr. Moore. It was you!"

"It was a fair exchange, as it turned out," Matthew Moore answered. "You and the other young ones just saved my life and brought me home!"

"How did you happen to come back to this part of Missouri?" Uncle Andrew asked, eager to have him tell the whole story.

"That's one thing I just don't know. Finally I thought I couldn't stay at that hospital one day longer. I had to start wandering. If I wandered, I might somehow get to a place where someone would know me."

"It must have been instinct that led you to these woods," Uncle Andrew said.

"Mama thought you were Daddy's ghost," Linnie said. "You sang that song, 'Sorrow, Sweet Sorrow,' didn't you? Did you leave the turkey and squirrels for us? Did you? And the little lame bird?"

"I'm still a little dazed, honey," Matthew Moore said. "It'll all come back, I know. All I do know now is that there was always something different in the air here—something that I knew. Now I'm home."

"Yes, Matthew," Mrs. Moore said, a prayer of thanks in her voice, "now you're home."

A Just Reward · 18

UNCLE ANDREW FELT deep concern for Matthew Moore. There was a great bump on his head, and his eyes were swollen and black. "I think Linnie and one of the boys should drive to town to get Dr. Manning," he said.

"Annie's the only doctor anyone ever used to need around here," Matthew said. "She can put a mullein poultice on my head and mix a sassafras tonic. In a few days, I'll be as good as new. There's never been a *real* doctor in White Hole Springs. He'd starve to death."

"There's a doctor there now, Matthew—young Seth Manning," Mrs. Moore told him.

"How did a Manning ever get to be a doctor? There

must be a dozen children in that family."

"There are, and six of them are working their way through high school at the School of the Ozarks. That's where Seth went. He did so well that a doctor in St. Louis backed him to go to medical school. Now he's come back to the hills to practice. That School of the Ozarks is a wonderful school."

"That's a fine thing for a boy to do," Matthew Moore said, "work to be a doctor. Mr. Belden, I don't need a doctor. All I need is to go to our cabin and rest. I feel real good. If you still think I need a doctor tomorrow, then Linnie can get him when you all go into town with these young people. Annie, I feel real proud of that money I saved. Since I've been at that cabin I've been digging ginseng, too, and I've got a good bundle of it stored away. It'll bring a good sum."

"Just to have you alive is all I want," Mrs. Moore told her husband.

"That Slim knew I had the ginseng," Matthew Moore continued. "He tried to steal it. Every time I saw him in the woods, I shot my rifle. That scared him off. He's nothing but a big coward and a bully."

"You can say that again!" Mart said.

Matthew Moore's voice grew stronger with indignation. "He stole that bait bucket, too, that belonged to the little girl. He tried to sell it to Mr. Glendenning. Mr. Glendenning is a good man. He had no time for Slim. After you young ones left the cabin that night, I took your bucket back to that cave. When you were away yesterday afternoon, I sat up there on the cliff with my rifle trained on the cave, too. I wasn't going to let Slim steal anything from you again."

"That's the miracle that kept Slim away afterward," Trixie said. "Oh, thank you, Mr. Moore. And you knew that we were at your cabin that night? Did you fire those shots?"

Matthew Moore's face saddened. "Yes. I fired them to scare Slim. He was in that woods. I wanted to keep him away from you. About the one thing that he's afraid of is a gun."

"That makes me ashamed," Trixie said. "I thought that bundle you had over your shoulder was my bait bucket and fish."

"It was my ginseng. I was putting it in my hiding place. It's still there, Annie. It'll help Linnie go to that school. I don't blame you at all, Trixie," he continued. "Slim tried all the time to throw suspicion on me. I only wish I'd known what he was up to before he set that fire."

"That's another thing that makes me ashamed," Trixie said. "I even thought at one time that you and Mr. Glendenning might have helped Slim set the fire. I saw someone lurking around the cabin that night, and I heard someone sing Linnie's song."

"I was there, all right. The song tormented me. I couldn't remember things. When I got back to my cabin, I smelled smoke and saw the glow of the fire. I hurried back with buckets and tried to wet the ground around the pines with water from the spring up there."

202

"Oh, Matthew, I told Trixie it was your spirit singing that song. . . ."

"Now, Annie," Matthew Moore said, "I hope we have a lot of years ahead before we turn to spirits. I'd like to go to our own home now, just you and me and Linnie together."

Jim, Brian, and Mart helped the injured man to his feet, and, leaning on them, he managed to walk to the cabin. Trixie and Honey followed the family, too excited at the remarkable turn of events to part from the "ghost."

When the boys had helped Matthew Moore to the rocking chair in the cabin living room, the Bob-Whites tactfully left the family to themselves. "We'll get our own dinner," Trixie told Mrs. Moore. "You just stay home with your husband and Linnie." Gratefully Mrs. Moore agreed.

"Gosh, I feel sort of scary," Mart said as they returned to the lodge. "It's as if a dead person had actually come back to life."

"That's practically true," Trixie answered. "Jeepers, when you think of all the things that have happened here!"

"And what has to happen yet before we get the reward for finding the fish," Brian added.

The boys insisted on going down to Ghost River for a last try at fishing. When they came back with a string of bass, Trixie and Honey had the pan ready for them on the big cookstove. Uncle Andrew, lured to the kitchen by the shouting and laughing he heard, offered to mix a salad of crisp wild greens, tender lettuce, and onions from the garden.

It was a happy group that sat at the table their last night at the lodge. The bass were golden brown. The salad was crisp and the dressing superb. They had young green corn plunged in hot water as soon as it was gathered and husked, and there were tiny pickled beets, mashed potatoes with butter, and, for dessert, a spicy deep-dish apple pie.

"Mrs. Moore made this pie, and she should have some of it for their dinner," Trixie said. "I'll just run over with some."

Uncle Andrew shook his head. "I don't believe I would. Mrs. Moore can make a *cordon bleu* dinner out of canned squirrel and poke greens. They need to be by themselves this evening. It's wonderful what's happened to them. Mrs. Moore has been so courageous all these ten years."

"Linnie, too," Trixie said.

Uncle Andrew nodded. "Things are going to be much better for the family from now on. You know, I'd gladly have helped send Linnie to the School of the Ozarks, but she'll be much happier the way it is. She'll have to work for part of her room and board. Everyone who goes there does that. And she'll have her father to help now, as well as her mother."

"Matthew Moore can't make a living digging ginseng and selling it, can he, Uncle Andrew?" Trixie asked with concern.

"Partly. There's a good price on ginseng. It's exported, mostly to China. The Chinese think it's a miracle drug that will cure everything. Aside from that, I need Matthew here at the lodge. Bill Hawkins would like to be able to spend more time farming his own place, and he'll be glad to turn his job here over to Matthew."

After dinner, the Bob-Whites washed the dishes and left the kitchen shining for Mrs. Moore in the morning. Then they went upstairs to pack.

The next morning, Matthew Moore, looking much younger with his hair and beard trimmed, insisted on harnessing the mules for Linnie. "It's marvelous to have my daddy here," she said. "Mama says we're a family once again. Are you all ready to go?"

"We'll never get on the plane with all the stuff we've collected here," Trixie said sadly and looked at a growing accumulation of bags and boxes being brought to the wagon. "We'll just have to leave all the spelunking equipment here."

"Do that!" Uncle Andrew said enthusiastically. "Then you'll be back next summer. Only next time, we'll explore the foothills and lakes and go easy on caves. I've hardly seen you except at breakfast and dinner."

"We'll do more rock hunting, too," Brian said. "There are minerals in these foothills that our government needs right now. I'd like to locate some of them. Jim and I have samples we're going to send to the

American Museum of Natural History when we get back to Sleepyside."

"Maybe you'll find your fortune in these Ozark hills," Uncle Andrew said seriously. "It wouldn't be too bad a place, either, for your school for boys."

"They could use some doctors around here, too," Brian said earnestly.

"And the Belden-Wheeler Detective Agency, too," Trixie said. "Don't forget that!"

"I'll *never* forget it," Uncle Andrew said.

"Some good advice about farming from Mart Belden, graduate agriculturist, would help, too," Mart said. "Jeepers, it'll be *years* before any of us finish college. By that time we may want to locate on the moon or Venus. . . . Someone help me lift this tank into the wagon, and we can be going. The famous Shem and Japheth Transportation System moves slowly. We still have a lot of business to look after and a train to catch."

The Bob-Whites said an affectionate good-bye to Mrs. Moore and thanked her for everything she had done for them while they were at the lodge.

"You gave Matthew back to me from the dead," she reminded them. "The thanks are all on my side. We'll miss you sorely, Linnie and me and my husband." Her eyes shone, and her face was flushed with happiness as she stood proudly beside Matthew and waved as long as she could see the wagon.

On the way to town they stopped for a brief good-bye to the Hawkins family. "Slim's in good hands now,"

Bill Hawkins said. "I delivered him to Sam Owens. We'll be looking for you next summer," he told the Bob-Whites.

"We've had a wonderful time, and we'll come back if we possibly can," Trixie said. "Thanks for everything, Mr. Hawkins."

In White Hole Springs the first person they saw was Sam Owens. "I had to take Slim to the jail in Laurel," he told Uncle Andrew. "Feeling was running too high around here for his safety. There'll be a quick trial. Then it'll probably be prison for him, and for a good long term."

"That takes care of that," Uncle Andrew said. "Now for the next order of business."

"I'm almost afraid to go over and talk with that magazine man," Trixie said.

"How could you miss, with two of each kind?" Mart asked. "The five hundred dollars is as good as in your pocket."

The editor of the *Scientific Digest* was excited when the boys set the small galvanized tank on the table in front of him. Quite a lot of people were standing around the room talking. Other tanks and bait buckets stood here and there on the long table.

"Do you actually have specimens of *Amplyopsis spelaeus?*" the editor asked. He brought out a big magnifying glass and held it close over the tank. "No one has turned up with true specimens so far. Come and have a look, Glendenning!" he called to the

Englishman, who was talking to two men at the other end of the table.

Trixie waited breathlessly as they watched the men examine the specimens in the tank they had brought. The editor looked at them from one side, then another. Then, with Mr. Glendenning, he carried the tank to the daylight in front of the window for better examination. Finally he turned and said sadly, "I guess we were expecting the impossible. The *Amplyopsis spelaeus* hasn't been found outside the Mammoth Cave in Kentucky. I was hoping to discover it here—to show, if possible, a continuation of the underground waterway from Kentucky through Missouri. Your fish may have museum value, and I am sure some cave in the Springfield area will be interested in buying them for exhibition. I'm sorry."

Trixie's face was white. She couldn't speak.

"Don't you care," Honey said, tears of disappointment in her own eyes. "We'll earn that money some other way when we get back home. You'll think of something, Trixie, just see if you don't."

"Maybe *I* won't," Trixie said proudly, "but the Bob-Whites will."

"That's the spirit!" Jim applauded. "That's *one* of the things I like about you. Say, what's Mr. Glendenning doing?"

"He's making some kind of a sign to that editor," Mart said. "He's motioning for him to go back and look at your tank, Trixie. Let's eavesdrop."

The men were in eager discussion, but their voices

were so low the Bob-Whites could hardly hear.

"It can't be!" the editor said, amazement in his voice.

"I tell you it is," Mr. Glendenning insisted, holding the magnifying glass close to the tank. "Don't you see the papillae in rows on the head and jaws?"

"Great guns!" the editor cried. "The *Troglichthys rosae!*"

"That's exactly what it is," Mr. Glendenning said. "Ruth Hoppin found it near Sarcoxie, Missouri, over fifty years ago. No one has found it since. Dr. Carl Eigenmann said the *Troglichthys rosae* has lived in caves longer and done without the use of its eyes longer than any living vertebrate."

"What does that mean to these young people?" Uncle Andrew asked.

"It means just this," the man from the magazine said. "They didn't find the specimens for which we offered the reward, but they have come up with something more rare. I have to talk to my board of directors, but I can promise this: It will bring a reward at least as great as that we offered for the Mammoth Cave fish. If the young people will leave us their address, we'll get in touch with them in about a week."

"Jeepers!" Trixie said, and she sighed a great sigh.

"Jeepers!" the Bob-Whites echoed.

"I know what you mean, and it's the way I feel, too," Uncle Andrew said, laughing. "Jeepers!"

Linnie hadn't said a word since they had deposited the tank in front of the editor. "I can open my eyes now," she said. "I've been praying under my breath all the time that you'd get that reward. I couldn't have stood it if you hadn't, after what you've done for Mama and me."

"Linnie, you're the very best friend anyone could ever have," Trixie said. "We're sure going to miss you."

"I feel just that way about all of the Bob-Whites." Linnie's face saddened. Then a big smile spread across it. "But not so much as I would have if my daddy hadn't come home. Say, isn't it getting to be almost time for your train?"

Mart glanced at his watch. "We should have just enough time to give the man our address—"

"I'll take care of that later," Uncle Andrew interrupted. "Here comes the train around the bend right now."

Mart scrambled to pick up his luggage. The other Bob-Whites picked up their bags and hurried after Mart.

The local train pulled into the station. Mart and Brian passed the luggage up to Jim, who stowed it away in the end of the dusty passenger car.

Smiling through tears, Trixie and Honey hugged and kissed Uncle Andrew and Linnie. The boys shook hands, helped the girls aboard, then swung up after them.

They waved till the platform faded from sight, then dropped into seats facing one another.

"Jeepers, things certainly happened fast today, didn't they?" Mart said. "My head's still spinning."

"Every day we were at Uncle Andrew's lodge things happened," Trixie sighed happily. "It's almost the best vacation we've ever had."

"Even if you did manage to get us into a lot of trouble," Mart said, "beginning when you ran out of the cave without telling anyone and got mixed up with that wildcat."

"But it wasn't my fault that Mr. Glendenning was dumped in the water and we had to save him," Trixie said defensively.

"Or that Slim did that awful thing to the bats in the cave," Honey said loyally.

"Slim sure was a pain in the neck," Mart added. "That fire he set could have destroyed the countryside for miles around."

"And a lot he'd have cared!" Brian pushed Mart over so he'd have more room in the seat. "He's where he can't do any more harm now."

"You can't blame Slim for the worst thing that happened," Jim said solemnly. "If you hadn't disobeyed rules, Trixie, you'd never have been so near death in that sinkhole in the cave."

Trixie's face grew very serious. She hated to have Jim displeased with her. Then a smile replaced the frown, and she winked mischievously at Jim.

"I know that was wrong. But a lot of nice things happened, too."

"That's right," Honey seconded her.

Jim smiled and nodded a vigorous agreement. "Of course they did, Trix," he said. "Nice things always happen wherever the Bob-Whites are. We met Linnie, for instance. That was one of the best parts of our vacation—right?"

"Yes, and we all love her," Trixie said happily. "Best of all, we *did* help restore her father to his family. Don't forget, too, that we found that ghost fish, and I *think* we're going to get a reward for it. That means we can help buy the station wagon for the crippled children, after all. Oh, dear, I wonder if we'll *ever* have another project as exciting as this one turned out to be!"

Trixie